Books in

The Human-Hybrid Project

series:

Яeflections
Silverback
of the

Яeflections of the Silverback

Farley L. Dunn

●●● THREE SKILLET

Published in Fort Worth, Texas

 THREE SKILLET

www.ThreeSkilletPublishing.com

Three Skillet Publishing
PO Box 162194
Fort Worth, Texas 76161

ISBN: 978-1-943189-95-3

First Printing October 2021/Printed in the USA

Яeflections of the Silverback

— Book 4 —

The Human-Hybrid Project

Bay City
Uptown East Side

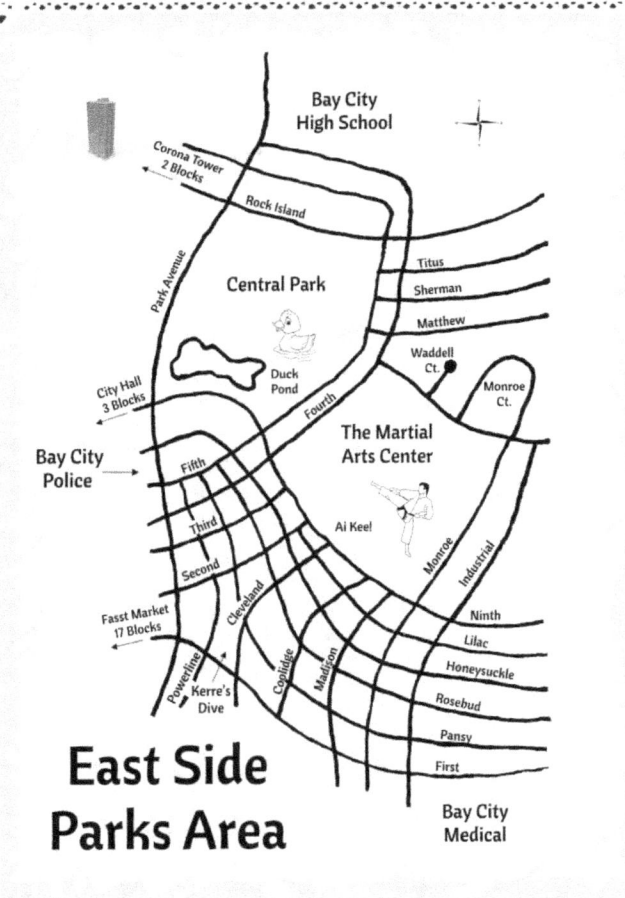

East Side Parks Area

Bay City
Old Town East Side

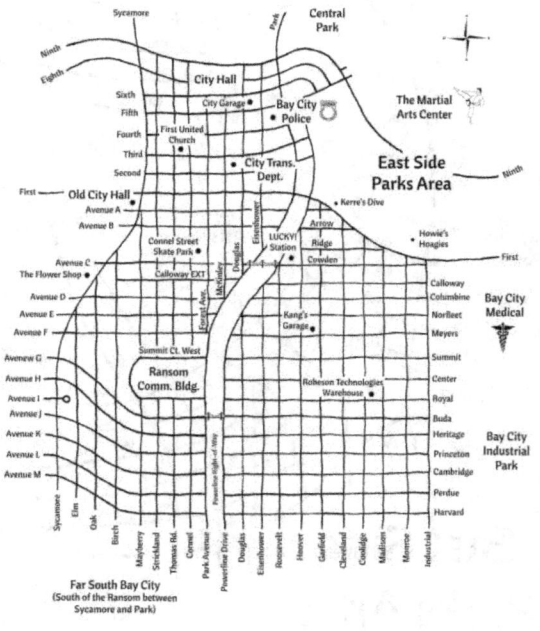

Bay City
Old Town West Side

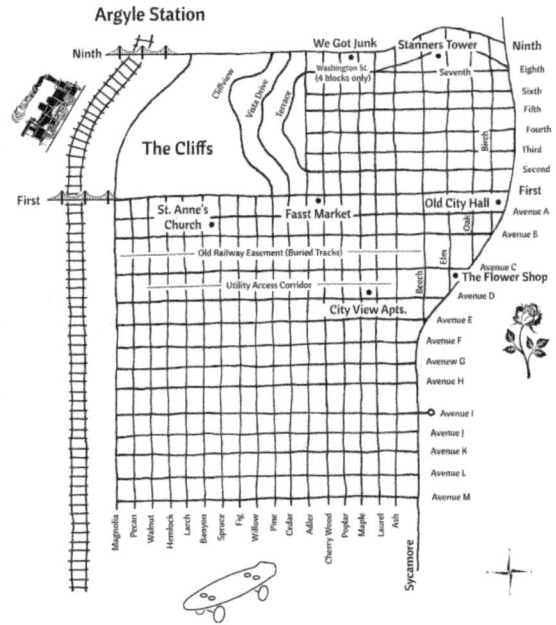

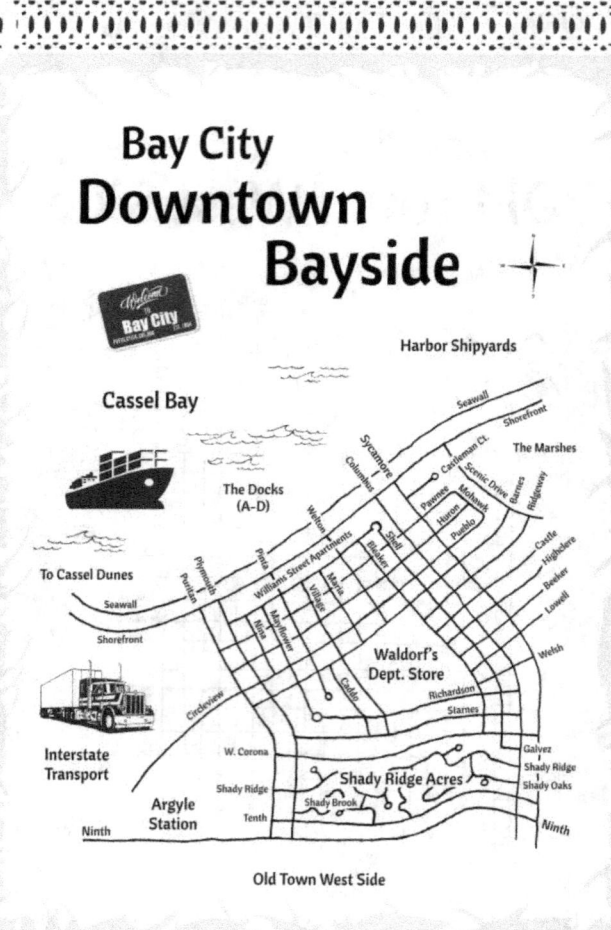

Bay City
Downtown
Bayside

Harbor Shipyards

Cassel Bay

Seawall
Shorefront
The Marshes

Sycamore
Columbus

The Docks
(A-D)

Castleman Ct.
Scenic Drive
Barnes
Ridgeway

Pawnee
Mohawk
Huron
Pueblo

Watson

Williams Street Apartments

Shell
Bicket

Pinta
Portsin
Plymouth

Nina
Mayflower
Maria
Village

Castle
Highadere
Becker
Lowell

Welsh

Caddo

Waldorf's
Dept. Store

Richardson
Starnes

To Cassel Dunes

Seawall
Shorefront

Crestview

Galvez
Shady Ridge
Shady Oaks

Interstate
Transport

W. Corona

Shady Ridge Acres

Argyle
Station

Shady Ridge

Shady Brook

Tenth

Ninth

Ninth

Old Town West Side

— I —

arik Shayk pressed his foot to the brake and located the shift mechanism. The burble of the transport van's engine took on a deeper tone and, hardly noticeable among the steady midnight hum of the city's power transformers, heat-exchange fans, and occasional sirens, the transport van with its twelve fugitives vanished through the roll-up door leading into the darkened bowels of the Ransom Communications Building.

One side of the van proclaimed it the property of The Martial Arts Center, and the other was marred by a shattered window. Inside lay Justin Kurtew, oozing blood and dead if he didn't get immediate assistance.

Two round circles of light revealed thick cables running up a corrugated surface. Racks of tools and metal lockers stretched into the darkness. Several doors with reinforced glass inserts and a cargo elevator emphasized the functional nature of the space.

Garik, who at 17 should be a senior at Bay City High, listened as the metal door rattled on its tracks, closing behind him, sealing them in. For months, he had been trapped in the basements of the Corona Tower, an unwilling participant in their secretive human-hybrid project. He now lived with timber wolf DNA in his veins. What he might evolve into frightened him.

He pictured Marisa, his girlfriend, his last words to her. *Run!* She believed he had been deported back to Russia, and there was Irina, his aunt, and his friends, Muhammad, Ibn, and Hayat, all jerked from his life, leaving him floundering.

"Garik, clothes?" A hand appeared at his window.

"Oh, right, Jantzen. Here, somewhere." Marisa became dash lights, a steering wheel, and the arm of a shirt on the stubby console. Jantzen had morphed—sublimated was more accurate, a closer technical term—into purple mist in order to enter the locked building and gain access to the underground parking garage.

Each time he did, he left his clothing behind.

Garik pulled a shirt and a pair of pants from underneath him and held them through the window.

"Thanks for the creases, my young friend." The hand wrapped the clothes in long fingers and disappeared.

"Anytime." Garik looked back into the van. The reflections of the headlights on the wall made his passengers into shadowed ghosts. "How's Justin?"

"Not better." Paolo Leveen, his hands dark with blood, held several fabric items against Justin's chest. He spread his fingers over the cloth to ensure even pressure, but it continued to ooze red.

"Lights." That was Joanie McDonald, vitreous-colored hair in a mohawk style, and tacit leader of the group. She could evaluate a situation and make a decision, earning her the position by rights. Her swagger was a visual reminder to anyone who forgot.

"Jantzen? Can we get lights?" Garik called through the window as he fiddled with the dash, searching. Jantzen had been driving before vanishing into smoke and leaving him to take the wheel. He had only ever driven his Street Strider, and the layout of the van's controls in the darkness was lost to him.

Jantzen must have been listening. The metal-on-metal thump of an industrial-size breaker reverberated, and smaller noises told of the overhead lights powering on, each one buzzing for a moment, then glowing deep red before beginning to brighten.

"The engine." Justin coughed, choking on blood and spitting. "Don't want to die . . . carbon monoxide . . . sorry." He coughed again.

"He's right. Kill it, though it's not his biggest worry." Jantzen appeared at the door with the broken window, now fully clothed, and he triggered the handle and slipped it aside. "We need to get him out."

Garik located the key and silenced the machine.

"Can we try a medical facility?" Paolo, who held the man's life in his hands—literally—looked out the windows at the industrial nature of the room. "The man's bleeding out."

"Bleeding yes, but not out," Jantzen reassured him, as the van began to clear.

John Carter, larger-than-life blond god, exited first, strapping a black-faced watch on his wrist. Now that they were away from the research center in the basement of the Corona Tower, he was certain he would have full access to the web.

Laura Lassere, wearing goth black, and Leigh Jose, in a second skin of leather, tumbled out after him. The relief of freedom was all over them.

Petite Amy Howe, oversized Julia Cantos, and lemur-like Marco Lopez exited together. Marco had a shine in his eyes. The room was a haven of climbable spaces, and he noted each one.

Alyna Lindberg, wearing retractable claws bequeathed by her Komodo dragon DNA, stayed to help with Justin, and she motioned for Giselle Harmon and Joanie to give them some space. The beautiful Giselle stopped beside Justin, made sure he was looking at her, and pursed her lips into a seductive kiss. She touched her fingertips to them and blew the kiss his way.

"Don't make him laugh," Alyna chided Giselle.

"I want Paolo to notice," Giselle hissed, and she softened it with a wink.

"How's he not, um, bleeding out?" Garik was still in the driver's seat, and he called to Jantzen, now leaning in and instructing Paolo and Alyna how best to move the man. He had thought *dying* but hadn't wanted to say it. Justin, DNA-bonded with a praying mantis, had taken on many of the mantis' extreme proportions, including thick forearms and extra joints. Now it seemed his skin was separating from his body.

What could cause that? An allergic reaction to your own skin? Garik cringed, wondering what his wolf DNA would eventually do to him. He'd watched werewolf movies, the horror of bones and sinews reshaping themselves under the full moon, the devastating conversion into full wolf form, becoming a monster that subsisted on other living creatures in the dark of the night.

Well, it was dark, and he *was* hungry. He ran his tongue along his teeth, relieved they hadn't changed while they were fleeing Corona Tower. Then, he remembered. There was no moon tonight. Arrgh! He might yet gnaw on the ankles of all his friends.

"Garik, are you with us?"

"Um, yeah?" He brushed his werewolf worries aside to find Justin already out of the van. Paolo and Alyna were helping him maneuver across the floor. The swelling of Justin's incipient wing structures bulged at his back.

"Are you planning to stay? The rest of us are headed inside." Jantzen had one hand on the upper part of the door opening, and the other on the handle ready to slide it closed.

"Sure, but what did you mean, Justin's not bleeding out? He's bleeding everywhere."

"Some of that is unavoidable. You saw the wings?"

"Sure." He'd watched Jantzen trying to make Justin more comfortable back in the basements. He'd been draining fluid from the bulging wing sacs.

"That's why Justin had to be rescued tonight. He's started to molt." Jantzen motioned with one hand, inviting Garik to join them. The others were disappearing into a door in the far wall.

"Molt?" Garik pictured a snake or a cicada. "Justin molts?"

"All good mantises do. Feel free to stay, but I'm turning out the lights when I reach the door." Jantzen closed the van's door, peered in through the broken window, and said, "Kevin's not going to be happy about this. I'm telling him I didn't break it."

"Jantzen, not fair!" Garik wailed as he threw back

his door and fell out. "You didn't give me the key!"

"I gave it to Giselle. Did you ask?" Jantzen was grinning.

Garik broke into a run just as Jantzen reached the door. True to his word, he flipped out the light. Trapped in the dark, Garik leaped and caught the door just before it closed.

Like a wolf would do, covering nearly twelve feet in a single arc of determination.

JUSTIN WAS wrapped in several roughly woven blankets with the Ransom logo stitched onto the fabric, likely designed for wrapping equipment while in transit. Leigh, the most altruistic of the group, knelt at his side with a bowl of water and a stained cloth. She sponged at the rips in his skin where they oozed red and yellow.

Paolo, after helping the man inside, struggled for focus, like he needed to be busy, but there was nothing he could do.

"Paolo, can I get you to help Giselle bring in my case? I've brought some things to help with Justin."

"Of course. I just, you know, would like to know if you have anything—"

"Have anything?" Jantzen's response said this was an old question.

Garik looked from Justin, shivering and breathing heavily, to Paolo, who was beginning to look almost as bad, to Jantzen, who seemed irritated at Paolo's question. Nothing about this made sense—well, the escape, perhaps, and he was happy about that, but he was now a fugitive, and that wasn't what he had imagined. The rest of this? There was a small kitchen and Alyna was heating water for coffee, Joanie had located a box of crackers, now opened, and John had inserted an earbud. He was off in a corner, peering out a blind and speaking into his watch.

Garik focused on Paolo, still pleading his case with Jantzen.

"So I can, you know, be there for Justin. In case, he, you know . . ." His words died away, and he fidgeted his hands.

"You're fine, and so will be Justin. With Giselle, please?"

"Sure, but anything for me?" He smiled hopefully.

"Alyna's doing coffee. That's a start. Don't fall off the wagon now, my friend."

"Sure, sure. Sugar, that works. Sugar, Alyna?" Paolo called, nearly pleading. "Lots, if you find any."

She called, "Feed the addiction, but yeah, I found some." She didn't look up, and she measured grounds and dumped them into the pot.

Giselle wriggled her fingers seductively at Paolo, pulling him forward with pursed lips, and she clicked on a large, black flashlight. "Pao, I really need your help. Now?"

Paolo sighed and headed her direction.

Jantzen stepped to Justin and knelt. "How long, do you think?"

"It's never been this bad before." He let out a bark of a laugh. "So, like, until I'm finished, okay?"

"Fair enough." Jantzen looked around at the others. "This is temporary. It belongs to the corporation, and they will eventually think to search here."

"I'm sorry I pulled you into this." Justin grimaced, and he tensed. The cracks in his skin became more pronounced, and new places began to seep. After a minute, he relaxed. "That one hurt. How do real mantises stand it?"

"You tell me. You're as real as they come. Leigh, keep him comfortable. Maybe he won't die."

"Maybe?" Justin lifted an arm, exposing an extra joint between his elbow and his wrist, balled his hand, and hit Jantzen on the knee. "So encouraging."

"Well, you didn't last time, so I'm holding out hope now." Jantzen stood, walked over to John and spoke to him a moment, before returning to Garik. "An adventure, hey."

"We're not really free, are we?" Garik had wanted out, his old life back. Riding his Street Strider, time on the roof with Marisa, wrapped in blankets against the cold of the night, and the skate park with his friends. "What will we do if they think to look for us here?"

"This isn't the only bolt hole in Bay City."

"Is it safe to stay here?" Bay City, he meant. Garik

thought of Christian. His precognition from his wolf-hound DNA-infusion hadn't protected him. He was shipped off, and no one had told him where. Weston Rodheimer and Halo Sunchaser, teamed up against all of them, seemed to have the power to root them out no matter where they hid. Garik didn't feel safe.

"Jantzen," Leigh called. "Something's happening. Get over here."

Justin let out a yell, and up and down his arms and legs, his skin began to bleed profusely. Garik pictured a mantis crawling out of its skin. When Justin crawled out of his, would Garik still recognize him?

He had seen the wings.

Garik looked at his own hands, once more reminded. He was no longer human, at least not a hundred percent. He wondered how long until it was his turn.

Then Justin yelled again, and his skin began to peel away.

$$— 2 —$$

antzen seemed the only one not in full panic.

Leigh pulled away the blankets and ripped one of them to staunch the flow of blood. Paolo and Giselle were just returning, and she called, "Giselle, do you have more cloth in that case?"

Paolo ran to them, removing his top and tearing the shirt in strips. He began helping Leigh wrap the uneven strips around the bloodiest parts of Justin's torso.

"We're here for you, buddy," he said, comforting Justin.

John had turned from the window. Even against the physical deformities each of them had witnessed as participants in the human-hybrid research project, Justin's calamity was a gut-wrenching wound in a life that had begun to tank from the moment of his infusion with DNA from his praying mantis cousin.

Leigh called, "He's burning up, John. Can you help cool him down?"

"Maybe." John could freeze his own blood, but could he transfer that to someone else? Practice in the basements of the Corona Tower had been theoretical, at best.

"Idea." Joanie, good at evaluating a situation and making decisions—the qualities that had elevated her into a position of leadership—stepped into the small kitchen and began searching for something to hold water. Under the counter, a bucket appeared, and she tossed it into the sink and began to fill it. She called to John, "Hands inside."

John nodded, slipped his sleeves up as he crossed the room, and thrust his hands inside as it was filling.

The bucket began to crackle with a surface layer of ice, and Joanie lifted it and placed it beside Justin. Leigh dropped in a folded cloth, cracked the ice, made a face when she touched the water, but squeezed the cloth to press out most of the liquid and placed it across Justin's forehead.

John shook the water off his hands. They were

bright red, and he wiped them against his pants to dry them.

"Now that the drama's played out, I need everyone to move back." Jantzen, with his slender face, dark hair and closely cropped beard, walked through the crowded space, motioning for everyone to give Justin room. "We can't stay here long, and Justin needs to get this over with."

What?!? Justin looked like he'd been pulverized by a meat grinder, and he was clearly in pain.

Garik had seen Justin as distant and critical and had fought him in an enforced challenge, barely beating the crazed hybrid in a show of cunning and force. Justin had also peeled back his raging bravado to reveal his damaged inner self, and how could Garik not understand that? He didn't consider him a *friend*, but he didn't look like he was going to survive whatever was happening to him, and to want him to *get this over with* just because his deteriorating condition was inconvenient?

Despite Jantzen's earlier assurances to Paolo, Garik's dismay overbalanced his self-control, and he blurted, "You want him to die faster?"

"Hardly, my young friend." Jantzen lifted his eyebrows. "Molt, remember? Or has your sense of adventure shocked your memory into senility?"

"Senility?" Garik heard himself repeat the word, appalled at how stupid it made him sound and embarrassed at his old habit. He reminded himself that getting angry would earn him nothing, even as he felt flayed inside. Still, senility was for old people, and it hurt that Jantzen used the word.

"He gets like that." Amy, with her hyper-fine down shimmering across her skin, leaned in and whispered to Garik. "But I think we should do as he asks."

"But Justin needs our help." Garik saw the others were doing as Jantzen had instructed, and he couldn't understand them not taking up Justin's case. Well, except Leigh, and she refused to move. She dipped another cloth into the bucket and squeezed it out before laying it on Justin's skin.

Jantzen squatted at Leigh's side, lifted one of Justin's arms, inspected the damage, and asked the bleeding man, "Is it bad?"

Justin grimaced, nodding his head.

"It will be over in a moment. Leigh, the cloths aren't necessary, but if you want to continue, they can't hurt. Just be prepared to move away quickly." Jantzen stood, took a deep breath, and explained the situation to the room. "As soon as the Tower registers the energy draw we're putting on this place, the puzzle will begin to fall in place for them—"

"Leave?" Joanie asked it like a question, but she nodded like it was a fact.

Alyna's hands flexed, and her razor claws gleamed for a moment before disappearing.

An odor arose from lemur-like Marco, and he raised one pawlike hand and whispered, "Sorry."

"Not again, little man!" Laura stood and moved away. "Do you have to scent every single place you wave your obnoxious tail?"

"I said I'm sorry," Marco repeated, but he fought a grin.

Justin jerked, and he cried out, not a word, but a call that shredded the soul. The guttural eruption was less human than animal, and all attention centered on the quivering form on the floor.

"Now, Leigh." Jantzen motioned to her that it was time. The cracked skin along Justin's arms and legs began to spit and shrivel, becoming a series of active volcanic fissures sending out red and yellow magma that instead of hardening, popped, burst, and splattered over everything within reach.

"Ew, Justin!" John was rolling down his sleeves. "That's nasty."

"Jantzen?" Paolo moved forward, as if to help, and only stopped when the bearded man motioned him back.

"Not now, Paolo. He only needs space." He looked around the room as though he wished he had more of it.

Giselle called to Paolo, simpering, "Pao? Hold me?"

He didn't seem to notice, or if he did, he intentionally ignored her.

Joanie was taking the bucket from Leigh when Julia cried, "Fire in the hole!"

Garik's head swam. They were all crazy! Sure, Julia was part constrictor, and she had the snake's ability to seek heat in the infrared spectrum, but fire in the hole? Did she see something funny in Justin's impending death?

Then Justin thrashed, his body cracked with a snapping sound, and he began to come apart, literally, like splitting a lobster shell to release the tender meat inside.

Only this time, the tender meat was Justin. Pus and blood, like molten volcanic excreta, flew everywhere.

"JUSTIN, NOT again!" Jantzen jumped backwards, as stringy goo flung itself over half the room and onto his clothes.

Again? Garik thought. How often had this happened?

Garik didn't get to ask his question, as Amy cried out, "Ooh!" and Giselle began liquifying in her chair. Marco leaped to the top of the upper cabinets above the kitchen sink, and John dove behind Giselle's chair.

Justin began to arise from his gooey sarcophagus of flesh, pulling out one arm at a time, and then his legs. He worked his head back and forth, until it snapped forward with a sucking sound. His torso lifted, thinner than ever, and stretching into something longer and bonier than Garik had ever seen. Even Julia was no longer tall by comparison.

His arms, with his extra joints and Popeye forearms, flexed, more armored flesh than skin. He snapped his jaws, clicking, before running a red tongue along his teeth. He growled, spat red to clear his mouth, and lifted himself to a standing position. His knees were bent, his arms held in front, and he turned his head back and forth to reveal large, glittering eyes.

Justin, yes, but not Justin, either.

Then he tensed, shivered, and wet, iridescent wings erupted from behind him. He knelt with one hand on the floor to steady himself as his wings extended to dry.

"Done, yet?" Jantzen had an edge to his question.

"About." Justin's voice came out a gravelly rasp, the sound of teeth grinding against teeth. He was breathing heavily, and he looked up and around the room.

Garik shivered at the predatory expression.

"Let me know when you can travel." Jantzen paused, perhaps waiting on Justin's acknowledgment. When the changeling didn't respond, Jantzen turned to the others. "The van is off limits. By now, they know it, and the damage would draw attention, anyway. Decide what's necessary, and that's what you bring. Only what you can wear or carry. Understood?"

The team nodded. Most had backpacks still in the van, with the bags carried by Julia and Leigh the exceptions. Gieselle's rolling case had provided room for Jantzen's things—and Gieselle's backpack. It sat on the floor, along with two other small packs for the men.

Garik still had his backpack of bottled water. After soaking the chair, Giselle was at the sink, diminished in appearance and throwing back glassful after glassful. Garik weighed the necessity of lugging the liquid around. Carrying it wasn't a problem. Whether he could replace it with something more important was a real concern.

"I have water in my pack in the van," he called out.

"Water?" Marco dropped from the overhead cabinet and scrambled over to Garik. "Giselle likes water. See? Thirsty!"

"It's good for washing off Marco's stink, too." Laura glared at him.

"I said I was sorry." Marco grabbed the end of his tail, worried it for a moment, then dropped it to scamper Justin's way. "Water, Justin? I can get you some."

"Sure, little guy. Go kill yourself." Grinding pops, bone moving in new and unusual ways, punctuated his words.

"Go kill myself. Funny, Justin." Marco rose onto two legs and moved with a remarkably normal gait to the small kitchen. He dickered with Giselle for a glass and water, and he returned it to Justin.

The wings had begun to shimmer, sheer sheets of mica, obscuring the wall behind, but barely. The air buzzed as Justin fluttered them. They looked completely inflated and mostly dry.

Jantzen sorted through the remaining things in the rolling case, and he carried a stack of clothing to Justin. At the bottom was a leather duster. It was the bulkiest of the items.

"We'll see if we allowed enough room for the wings." Jantzen shook out the duster.

Garik understood. It was full through the torso, much too much for Justin's thin frame. However, when Justin folded his wings—which Garik was certain he could—the duster would fill out perfectly, giving him a normal, perhaps even muscular look.

Blending in with the natives, so to speak.

Amy and John had returned to the van. The door was open, and the lights from the garage laid a skewed rectangle of light on the floor. Laura and Joanie followed them, Joanie's voice offering clipped suggestions that weren't really suggestions. Leigh was helping Justin clean away the remains of the mucus and other goo, while Paolo helped Justin work his newly long body into his fresh clothes.

Garik shrugged. His water comment had seemed to disappear into the busyness in the room, and he moved to the garage, searching for a way to help. Under the bright lights, the van was surrounded by the things everyone had carried. His backpack of water held up a concrete post, the box Alyna had carried was now emptied, and Joanie was working the items into two nearly full backpacks. The escape hadn't gone exactly how he'd expected, and he hadn't been a successful participant. Breaking the van's window. He wanted to hit himself in the head. *Ask, Garik. That's all you had to do.* It had felt he was doing something brilliant in the moment. Now, they could no longer use the van, and it was his fault. He heard feet on the concrete at his side, and he smelled Marco without looking.

"That was something in there, wasn't it? Nobody else does that, molting, not me, anyway. I change sl-*oo*-wly. What do you think you'll do? Quick or slow?"

Garik didn't want to think about it, and he kept his focus on the activity in the underground garage.

"Lemur got your tongue?" Marco snapped two slender, lemur-like fingers in front of Garik's face.

"That's stupid." Garik pushed the hand away.

"Oh, wolf boy is in a bad mood." Marco fell to all fours, darted to Garik's other side, and stood, his long snout barely above Garik's shoulder. "Let me tell you a bad mood. Wait until you're compelled to scent every flowerpot in the room. That'll give you a reason for a bad mood—"

A siren and flashing overhead lights cut off Marco's whining tirade. Faces glanced up, and the final members of their squad burst through the door into the underground garage. Justin wore a knit beanie in black pulled low over his head, on one hand deemphasizing his outsized cranium and on the other setting off his wide eyes and elongated jaw. In his duster, at a glance, he seemed mostly human. His hands were covered by black mittens—not gloves, Garik noted. What had his hands looked like after he molted? Garik wasn't sure, but not five fingers.

"Booby trap." Marco grinned as Joanie yelled for each person in the game to shoulder a bag.

Forget trading out what was in his pack. He was taking *something*. Garik wasn't making another mistake, and the pack filled with water was the only thing he knew for certain to be his.

Then the door began to rumble with the repetitive metallic clack of a chain-driven opener. The controls beside the door were ominously unattended. It was being manipulated from outside.

Garik's stomach twisted. Personal failure or not, they had escaped the Tower. To be recaptured skewered him.

Marisa! He was so close to home. Not again!

— 3 —

lyna yelled, "Bushwhackers, all! Let 'em come. I'll take 'em all out."

Her claws were fully extended, and they gleamed like silver knives, chromed carbon, nightmares that whispered death in the dark.

"Something better," Leigh said, her voice cracking with pain. She frowned, her face twisted, and she turned to each wall in the room, pausing as though searching. She rubbed her temples. "Julia," she called, "my ultrasound says there are hollow spaces in the wall, deep ones that lead away from here."

"Tell us where." Julia had her pack ready, and she stood with it already across one shoulder.

"I, I can't focus. Too much is happening. My head hurts." Leigh's face crumpled. She was right about the "too much." The large room now struggled to contain more action than a kindergarten classroom on a party day.

Laura wrapped an arm across her shoulders, consoling her with, "Quit trying so hard. Let us help you."

Garik wasn't sure how he heard that. With the noise of the rising door, and people scrambling to gather what they could cram into backpacks that suddenly seemed too small, the hard-walled space echoed with ear-splitting noise. At least it was unimaginably loud to Garik. No one else seemed to mind.

Air moved, warmth feeding from the back wall. He realized it was cold outside—as he was reminded by the wall of frozen darkness sweeping under the rising door—but the large space had been warm when they had returned to gather their things. He listened carefully. He could hear the air moving, a repeated clicking that could be a loose grille. He glanced at the door, now revealing headlights slowly sweeping across the sill plate, ready to rush in and haul them back as one and lock them up on Basement Level 5 with the disappointing rejects from the human-hybrid project's latest discarded has-beens.

Garik didn't want to be a has-been. He wanted his freedom back. They had stolen that from him, and it was no longer theirs to have and to hold. He would fight for his and for the freedom of those with him. They were a kind of family, now, and he would battle for them at risk of his own life.

He hoped they felt the same about him.

The first man that leaned in to look underneath the door got a spray of aromatic scent from Marco. He screamed and ducked away.

"They should know better." Marco grinned.

"Least it's good for something," Laura called out. She yelled over the noise, "Ideas? I can kill a few, but that's not going to look good on our record."

Jantzen stood beside Amy, a neatly groomed statue. He looked as if he'd changed clothes after Justin's volcano. He said, "Are you tracking them?"

"Each one," Amy said, without moving. The hairs on her skin rippled, a windswept continent of knowledge. Her eyes blazed with a hundred images, each of someone or something different.

"How long?" Before they breached the door, he meant.

"I don't think they mean to hurt us. None have weapons ready." The incoming night whipped at her clothing. She shivered.

"So, how long?"

"Not long enough," she said. "And there's nowhere

to run."

"Yeah. Stopping here was maybe not brilliant."

Garik was appalled. Jantzen, giving up? No! They had to protect each other, fight, do *something!* He called to Julia, "Behind the van, there's heat. Can you locate the source?"

"A vent?" She was tightening the straps on Leigh's pack, and she gave a strap a yank and moved to the end of the van. "I found it. Leigh, can you tell how big it is?"

"Let me get closer."

Justin blocked her way, and his eyes glittered. His head turned to survey the panic overtaking the room, a swivel for a neck, his head tilting at angles no human neck could manage. His jaw released and snapped shut, the battle-ready response of a warrior-bred fighter.

"Justin, move!" Leigh put her hand on his arm and stepped underneath. He jerked away, stood taller, and clacked his teeth.

"You just had to ask." A clattering growl.

Leigh knelt at the wall, and she and Julia began pushing things aside. Paolo understood and joined them, muttering, "I'm here to help, if you want it."

"Of course, you lug." Julia handed him a bulky roll of insulated wiring, and he tossed it to the side. It hit a good distance away, bounced once, and rolled to beside the van before falling over.

Taunts from the darkness were garbled locks and

keys, an onslaught of bravado about to wash in under the door, and yet, even in their indistinct threats, they still managed to say, "We've trapped you! Boo-ya! No sense in running now!"

Clearer, Garik caught an undercurrent of voices, one he remembered from his first moment of awareness in the research hospital. *"You were deported right back to Russia where you could no longer cause our good country additional problems. No one will come looking for you."* He shivered at the memory of Weston Rodheimer's mocking tone. The man had no heart, no compassion, no leniency. Either you joined his team, or he cast you aside.

Garik didn't want on his team. Maybe no one had come looking for him, and maybe they had. He'd never know if he didn't escape this basement parking garage. He pictured Marisa, and his eyes watered with the wasted months he'd been imprisoned in the Corona Tower basements.

Then he focused on what Rodheimer was saying.

"Yes, there's a service tunnel under the street. It runs under Park to the powerline right-of-way. Get men over there now. If Jantzen discovers it first, we may have a real chase on our hands."

"Jantzen," Garik called, wishing he hadn't distracted Julia and Leigh with the heating vent. Leigh's ultrasound ability was crucial to sorting out the missing escape route. "There's an underground service tunnel."

Joanie called, "John, Giselle, our plan. Get the others. Where?" She aimed her final word at Garik.

Jantzen still stood by Amy, and he called to Garik, "You know this how?"

What!? He had time to ask that? "Rodhemier's outside. He's sending someone to guard it. It runs under Park."

Jantzen looked toward the east wall of the garage. Three doors gave them three options. He seemed to hesitate.

Amy called, "Time's up. They're coming in."

"I've got this," Alyna yelled. "Everyone, after me."

Her claws glistened, shadows of obsidian at the tips of her fingers. At the first door, she pressed her hand to the door, leaned into it, and her claws buried themselves. She twisted her arm, pulled back, and a third of the door tumbled to her feet. Inside, a porcelain sink and a toilet gleamed.

"Again," Joanie called. She wore two packs, one on each shoulder, and pulled Justin along beside her.

The second door proved a better option. Alyna used both hands, sinking them into the metal like butter, and the door dropped away like a day-old waffle, bent and battered, and about as useless. A corridor disappeared into the darkness.

"Inside," Joanie yelled. She didn't care about the third door. She had evaluated the situation and made her decision.

She was right to hurry everyone along. The overhead mechanical door, rolling up into its metal cage, although slow, now allowed a full view of the Tower pursuit team. Military vehicles from the Tower's basement parking garage filled the street. Spotlights leaped into action, liquid swords of light piercing the inside of the Ransom Building's underground garage, prepared to slice and dice anyone they found.

Garik didn't want to be found. He didn't want to be sliced and diced, either. He'd had enough of that.

Alyna ducked inside the newly opened doorway, her claws sheathed, and a pack in her hands. John was on the way with Giselle, and they disappeared into the darkness after her. Marco scampered in on their heels, leaving a trail of fear behind him. Amy and Jantzen held their position, Amy pointing out the location of each of their pursuers. Leigh pulled down on Justin's shoulder, suggesting his new height might be a problem in the dark passageway. It was something she could *see*, her dolphin ability to navigate the unknown.

Garik knew he was fast, faster perhaps than anyone else in the room, and he calculated the various bags and packs left behind. His water by the concrete post, he didn't how soon they would have access to more, even in the city, and he remembered Alyna's words: Giselle might need some if she had to squeeze through a tight space. Rehydration afterward would be vital.

More laser pulse than boy, more live electricity than

runner, more lightning strike than any human ought to be, Garik was a tornado, snatching up the items, checking off one at a time as he slipped his arms into straps or grabbed waiting handles. He noticed how everyone else seemed to slow down, mired in a psychedelic glow as he ran, but his focus was on escape, not the blurred sense of time dilation that seemed to fog the corners of the room with the remnants of pale rainbows.

The items didn't even seem heavy in the exhilaration of his whirlwind flight across the space. He owed that to his practice in the pool, the repeated laps and breathing exercises overseen by Christian. He felt he could run from Argyle Station on one side of the city to the other and never slow down.

Julia, with her dark demeanor and her stealthy way of moving without seeming to move, paused before entering the passageway to give Joanie access. Garik thought, *Move. We're out of time.* He had seen the teams heading in, the BolaWraps at their waists. He'd had one used on him, and he didn't recommend the experience.

A blast of sound rattled the lights overhead. Amy grabbed her ears, and in the concussion, Jantzen evaporated into purple mist. The two windows in the van closest to Paolo cracked, then they shattered inward. The military team entering the building dropped their weapons like molten metal, and they fell to their knees, pushing their helmets off to yank out earpieces and clutch their ears.

Amy looked dazed when the noise faded. Paolo stood wide-eyed, with surprise on his face. The remains of Jantzen were no more than wisps of purple fading into the night.

"Not again," Amy said, as she shook her head clear and knelt to pick up his clothes. "He'll want these. Out, Paolo. That way." She pointed to Joanie beside the damaged door.

Garik waited, still unsure what had just happened. Joanie stopped Paolo at the door.

"You?"

He nodded, shrugged and managed to look embarrassed.

"How?" Joanie blocked his way, expecting more of an answer. On the other side of Paolo, the men in camo had started to stir.

"Not now," Amy said. "He's given us the time we need," and she pushed past with Jantzen's clothes in her hands.

"I didn't know I could," Paolo said, almost to himself, and he slipped through the door, hot on Amy's heels.

"Didn't know he could." Joanie shook her mohawk in dismay. Then she looked at Garik. "You, get along. Leaving this place behind."

It was a near sentence, so Garik figured she meant it. He hitched up his bags, and he lit off into the darkness, wondering what mysterious skill he would suddenly discover he could do.

And would he like it? Or would it be something he'd wish away for the rest of his life?

He let the thought fade. Somewhere ahead was their hope of escape. He just prayed they found friends on the other side.

THE PASSAGE seemed a black hole of endless night, but they tumbled through the door on the far end after only a few hundred feet.

They stood near the top of Stanwick Hill. The door they'd exited left them in the middle of the powerline right-of-way under a star-studded sky. The industrial park entrance and the Bay City Medical parking lot glowed ten blocks to the east. Kang's Garage was only blocks away on Meyers, if Garik could find the sign. It wasn't lighted this time of night, and he knew better than to waste time looking.

The grassy right-of-way—with thick ropes of powerlines running overhead—cut through town for over twenty blocks, ending at First, where the lines dove underground, spreading their electrical roots to nourish the city's hungry buildings. Garik recognized Powerline Drive just past the right-of-way, although it was an asphalt wasteland at this hour. He and his friends had often taken the long way from City View Apartments—catching the light to cross at Sycamore and taking the Avenue G bridge at Park over the right-of-way—just to jump the curbs all the way to The Martial Arts Center, Central Park, and Corona Tower beyond.

The wind in his face, the thump of his trucks as his board ground along the concrete curbing, the speed of flight—even if it was mostly on wheels. He could taste it, and he wanted it back again.

The Avenue G bridge from Park to Powerline Drive was only two blocks to the south. The other way, the nearest bridge over the wide expanse of the right-of-way was six blocks north at Avenue C. He remembered Rodheimer's words. *"Service tunnel ... runs under Park to the powerline right-of-way ... get men over there now."* It was clear over which bridge they would first see the threat of capture.

"This way," Garik called, raising a hand he was certain no one could see in the darkness. "I know this city, and we need to get away from that bridge."

He pointed to the Avenue G bridge where the street turned into Buda Road, and as he spoke, headlights pooled on the bridge, forming frozen lakes of white. Slamming doors told of dark-suited men on the prowl.

"Garik?" A familiar voice rang crystal clear through the stillness of the cold night air from the direction of Powerline Drive.

"Muhammad?" The familiar voice offered a lifeline to Garik, reaching in to massage his heart and emotions.

At that moment, he needed Muhammad—all his friends, but especially the one he could hear right then —more than life or escape.

"Hey, you dundersap! You back to stay?"

"I never went anywhere. Hold up! We're coming your way."

Garik was aware of the cautions being thrown at his back. Jantzen hadn't appeared yet, Marco was scrambling around in the grass, joyous just to be outside, and Leigh was painting a picture of three people she clearly sensed and for Garik to use caution, but he didn't care. Muhammad Saud was his friend, and he wouldn't be with anyone who would bring him harm. His friendships—every one—had been stolen from him, and he intended to make this his night to throw an arm across someone's back, crack an old familiar joke, and learn if Marisa had missed him as much as he still missed her.

He hiked his packs, hailed his escapees with a "Follow me," and tore across the grass, certain this was the start of his journey home.

— 4 —

y best brother! Allah be praised!" Muhammad clapped his arms around Garik in a quick but firm hug. He backed up, looked into his friend's face, and blurted, "Dundersaps, don't do that again."

"What? Do what?" With his friend's ribbing, Garik's clock wound backwards, and the months underneath the Corona Tower had never happened. *Muhammad!* They were together again, something he didn't know how much he'd missed.

"Go off and leave us. You broke Marisa's heart,

you goof." Muhammad pulled off his ever-present skullcap with its skull stitched into the fabric and hit Garik in the chest with it before slipping it back onto his head. "You out to see what's going on at the Tower? News is all over the city!"

"Yah, about that—" Garik barely got the words out before yet another familiar voice accosted him.

"Nyet, my disappearing friend. It is my turn to say welcome back to my Russian comrade." Out of the dark, Ibn Hariri's face appeared, and he held up a hand. Garik threw his up also, and they clasped fists forearm to forearm before releasing hold.

"Your beard, Ibn. It's not so scraggly as it was." Garik laughed. "Someday, perhaps, you'll make a man."

"My dreads say more. I am fully a man. No one can say otherwise."

"Except his girlfriend." A third face, fresh to the group, leaned in, ribbing Ibn. He held a skateboard with a Baker Brand logo, shifted it to one side and extended a hand. "Dieter. So, this is the most, how do you say, infamous friend. You found the basement. Amazing! No one else we know can do that. Ha, ha. You are a good friend to have around."

"Deet," Ibn elbowed him, "no one can know."

"Can know what?" Justin emerged behind Garik, recognizable in the dark by his height and his black leather duster. His question snapped at the end like oversized teeth being clacked together, or the beak of an insect, ready to rend its supper into more manageable tidbits.

"These are my friends, Justin. That's Muhammed with the skull, and the dreads is Ibn. The new one is Dieter."

"Ah, all are new to me." Clack, clack. "We have friends following us. Perhaps *your* friends could help us make our way to safety."

Dotting the powerline corridor, small circles of light bobbed in the darkness, revealing the remains of summer's long dead and dissected grass. The Avenue G overpass where it turned into Buda just to the south revealed a spotlight warming up on the back of a military transport, and six blocks to the north towards Corona Tower, lights flickered on the Cowden Street overpass. The pincher action of the Tower's long arms was about to close them in.

"Move. Now." Joanie shouldered Garik and Justin aside and zeroed in on the three city youths. "Willing to help?"

"Um, sure. How?" Muhammad took charge, wrapping his friends into the excitement, as teen boys will do.

"Someplace to hide." John appeared out of the darkness, his hair and Nordic coloring highlighting him with a wintry brush. "Garik seems to trust you. We must, also. But it happens now, or *they* win." He used his long arms to indicate the two bridges.

From the looks on Ibn's and Dieter's faces, the thrill of something exciting in Bay City was enough. Garik relaxed as a purple shadow painted Jantzen's outline in the darkness.

"Amy!" Garik called. "We need clothes!"

She pressed them into his hand, and Garik held them out to the mist. He shook his head at how often this was happening as they vanished from his hand.

"I appreciate these." The purple mist winced with pain as Jantzen coalesced into something real. "You think this would be fun, if it didn't hurt so much. I've left misdirection for our pursuers, but we must be gone. Justin, can you fly, yet? We need reconnaissance."

"I can try." The tall man awkwardly slipped off his duster and tossed it Jantzen's direction. His skin glowed in the darkness, the sheen from the distant lights glinting on his too-bony flesh. He straightened, and his torso elongated. Against the starry sky, he became more mantis than man. His teeth clacked, the extra joints in his forearms snapped menacingly, and with a shake of his shoulders, his wings swelled against the night. They began to buzz with action, disappearing except for the sound, and within moments, he was aloft.

"Dundersaps," Muhammad whispered.

"Holy moly," hissed Ibn. "Better than Jezebel and the Sticks."

"Is very cool, yes?" Dieter seemed to be having the

time of his life. "Wait till Papa hears about this."

"Nein." Garik looked at the three new members of their fleeing group of refugees, deciding he had to take charge of this before it got out of hand. "Got that, Dieter?"

"These are your friends, I trust?" Jantzen was buttoning his shirt.

"If they can keep their mouths shut."

"Good. You, with the skull, we need to hide. What are our options?"

"I'm Muhammad," he grinned, "and Dieter and I have a really good idea. Follow us."

And now they were sixteen.

"TELL ME about Marisa." Garik's arms wrapped his backpack, and his body vibrated to Ibn and Dieter's boards up and down a wood halfpipe. The back of Muhammad's head tapped the boards with each run of the skaters' wheels up and down the pipe.

"Missing you. Like, the lights went off when you left. Man, I never expected you to just up and disappear."

"Me either, Mo." Garik let his eyes rove the warehouse rising like a shell around them, shielding them from the darkness and their pursuers. It belonged to Dieter, well, not exactly Dieter, but it was for Dieter's use.

Dieter lived in the Tower, *in the Tower!* with his

father. The reason why, though, was like biting into an apple and finding half a worm after you swallowed. His father was under supervision at the Corona Cancer Center, and he had wanted a place for his son to chill on the days he was taking treatments. At Dieter's encouragement, he had rented the warehouse at Coolidge and Royal and had the ramps and other things built for his son.

Dieter's father hadn't known about the Connel Street Skate Park, Muhammad whispered with a gleeful grin. Otherwise, they wouldn't have this place to play in. Muhammad leaned his skateboard into his lap and spun one set of wheels. "Outside, I might not'a known ya' if it hadn't been dark."

"What!?" Garik laughed and stuck his hand into his hair, working his fingers in. It was long enough to do that now. "You couldn't see me no matter, so how could being dark help?"

Alyna sat across the room. Garik bet she could recognize people in the dark. Her eyes were closed, but he bet she knew everything going on around her. Justin had crashed beside her. He had returned—after an hour—exhausted, revealing that the Tower's search was centered on the powerline right-of-way, and Dieter had found him a box of trail bars to chew on. The wrappers scattered the floor around him.

"Still wondering why you cut off your hair."

"That." Garik pulled his hand away and looked at it.

"I didn't—"

"It didn't cut itself, dunderdude." Muhammad punched him on the shoulder.

"Yeah, I know. You should have seen it at first. It was nearly shaved. It's just now feeling real again." He remembered it bristling against his pillow and his dismay that they had *cut his hair!*

"Mostly it's your eyes." Muhammad pressed his palm against the spinning wheel, and it stopped. Even hearing the repeated and loud reverberations from the skateboards, the sound of that one wheel stopping seemed to silence the world.

At least for Garik.

"What about my eyes?" How many months had it been? Last summer, at least, and now it was cold outside. His hair had grown inches. Yet, he'd stood in front of the mirror that first day he'd been awake, and he'd studied his reflection. His eyes, how had they looked? Like always, he recalled. No difference, he wanted Muhammad to say. Ah, Garik, they look just the same. I'm just pushing your buttons.

Garik had just seen Justin *molt* and change into something different than he was before. He knew *he* wasn't the same, either. Timber wolf DNA. What made timber wolves special? Strength enough to break open bones to eat the marrow inside. He'd learned that on the nature channel. They were survivors that could live almost anywhere, survive in almost any conditions.

Speed, able to cover fifteen or more miles at a time, at up to thirty miles-per-hour. Endurance. Cooperation with the pack. Oh, and they morphed into werewolves when they shared a human half.

Just pushing your buttons, Muhammad. That's what I want you to say.

"Aw, nothing." Muhammad grinned and pulled his cap off to inspect the skull before slipping it back on again. "Deet keeps extra boards under the pipe. Been on yours much?"

"Some." Garik didn't want to say it had been an electric one. Electrics were for posers. Real skaters powered their own.

"Here. Borrow mine. I'll use one of Deet's."

Garik took the board in his hand, rubbing his fingers over the familiar blood splatters covering the top and the skull on the bottom, and he felt the world was right again. Like it should have been all along.

He still wanted to know about Marisa—and his eyes. What was Muhammad not saying about his eyes?

Then he shrugged. He had a skateboard in his hands, and he had a halfpipe at his back. It was time to have some fun.

GARIK LAY awake, his eyes following the structural supports forming the ceiling of the old warehouse. Long strings of lights ran down the center, now off so people could sleep.

After an hour of skating fun, Dieter had claimed his father as an excuse to leave, saying his papa would be "unpleased" if he was out until daybreak. It was no problem for them to stay in the warehouse, however, as his papa rarely made an appearance. The code to the door was their invitation to come or go as they pleased.

Garik had given Muhammad a slap on the back and Ibn a fist bump, and they had headed back to their homes, Muhammad at his grandmother's and Ibn with his parents. The warehouse had an old breakroom with a small kitchen and a half bath, with both in their original condition. Beggars couldn't be choosers, and the escapees from the Tower had cleaned up and found corners to wrestle makeshift bedding out of backpacks and several builder's tarps left over from the construction of the indoor skate park.

Now, morning light tried to sneak in under the door to the small office that held the only windows in the vast building. The office was boxed out of one corner, only reaching halfway to the ceiling. Dieter's father had pushed the halfpipe next to it, added a loft at each end that covered the office at one side and housed the kitchen and half bath at the other, and a tight stair gave access to the loft. Wooden rails, steel benches, and drop-ins with a bowl off to one side filled in the rest. They now served as nests for the individuals on the run.

Garik was awake because of his dreams. *Nightmares.* His eyes. He kept seeing Weston Rodheimer's face, the man's strangely unusual eyes boring into him. White, white eyes, covered by contacts that kept slipping sideways to reveal nothing there except blank white orbs. Then Rodheimer's skin began to crack and fall away—*molting!*—and his broad shoulders turned into the hairy shoulders of a gorilla, one bigger than Garik had ever seen.

"You," Rodheimer had said in his dream, "are like me, a changeling. What will you become, my young friend? I need you back before your molting begins. I will find you, and I will help you discover what your future can be."

Garik didn't want to molt. He wanted what his life used to be—except Arik, perhaps. If he could have his old life back without his aunt's boyfriend, that would be perfect, but he'd take Arik if Rodheimer would let him go.

Then the gorilla man had put his thumbs to his face, forced his eyes from their sockets and held them out to Garik, saying, "With these, you will see what you can truly become."

Garik had covered his face to protect his eyes, and that's when he had jerked awake, his heart pounding in fear and unable to settle back into sleep.

His eyes. What had Muhammad seen there? Garik felt sorry for Justin, and he wondered if Justin felt sorry for himself—or if the changes sat well on his shoulders, what was left of them, anyway.

Rodheimer, what DNA combination had given him those shoulders and eyes? Some dogs had really white eyes. Surely not—

The despair of the possibilities drenched Garik with emotion, and he fought to keep his body under control. He didn't want to become what Rodheimer had suggested. What if they had been mistaken, if Dr. Jimenez and Nurse Ratchett had given him gorilla DNA by mistake, and that was the reason he had never acquired Christian's precognitive abilities?

Maybe his eyes were gorilla eyes, and that's what Muhammad had seen.

He sat up, listened to the sound of the rousing city just beyond the walls, and he navigated his way to the small restroom, stepping inside and closing the door before turning on the light. The exhaust fan roared, and he was glad. He let himself sink into his despair, attempting to choke back a sob before it overtook him.

When it was done, he wiped his face, looked into the mirror, and tried to see what Muhammad had seen. He couldn't tell. Maybe he'd forgotten what his eyes used to look like. What had Muhammad said? He wouldn't have known him if it hadn't been dark.

At least his voice hadn't changed. What did a gorilla sound like? How about a timber wolf? Could he pretend to be either one, and could he convince anyone if he did?

After his first few attempts, someone banged on the

door. "That you, Peach Fuzz? Howling at the moon? Restroom's for all of us."

"Out in a minute, Joanie."

Garik grinned. At least he could guess which he was better at, even if his dream had made one seem more real than the other. And he remembered Joanie's remark the first time they had spoken. *Too human.* It had felt like a put-down then, but he was glad for it now.

No thanks, Mr. Rodheimer, you can keep your gorilla. I don't want any part of it.

Still, he investigated his reflection in the mirror and checked the set of his shoulders. Wider? Not that he could tell. His jaw, chunkier? Not yet. He also didn't have extended canines, but those could come from a gorilla or a wolf.

The door pounded again, and Garik sighed, turned from the mirror, opened the door, and called, "Next!"

$$— 5 —$$

second reconnaissance flight by Justin was out of the question, and Muhammad, Ibn, and Dieter had classes at Bay City High. They wouldn't be of any help until later that afternoon.

The bigger issue for the moment was food and supplies. The warehouse—a boon!—gave them anonymity from the city's prying eyes, but it wasn't equipped to house thirteen people for an extended time. Going outside was possible, but if they were spotted by cameras or, heaven forbid, drones, the Tower would be on them like ants on a drop of honey.

Marco volunteered before anyone even asked.

"I need snacks. I assign myself as the getter of supplies. Money? Anyone? I didn't bring any." He sat up, his tail flicked, and he worked his mouth back and forth in a manner that made him seem more lemur than little man.

"And how are you planning to manage that?" Jantzen, somehow impeccably dressed with his hair and beard flawless, dropped down the distance from the loft to the floor, landing lightly, and becoming bigger with his question than his physical body suggested.

"Just *go*. No one cares, Jantzen. I'm out, then back, so quick. Who is there to see?" Marco waggled his fingers and grinned. "Maybe a little five-finger discount."

"I'll do it." Laura had been sorting her things from a backpack. She stood and looked over the group. "I'm pretty normal—"

"For a goth queen." Marco snickered.

"You, you—" She darted his direction with her hands prepared to grab his neck.

"Enough of that." Jantzen tried to hold back a sigh, not entirely successful. "John, Giselle, how about you?"

"Sure—" John began when he was interrupted.

"Better idea, Jantz." Giselle smiled impishly, and she raked her eyes up and down John. "Such a tall boy, and so *Nordic*. The man stands out like a lighthouse. Send Leigh with me. We can be two silly schoolgirls out skipping classes for the day. No one will think anything of that."

Jantzen seemed to consider it, waiting on John for input. John gave way with a, "Fine, then," and he glared at Giselle, "if you think anyone will believe you're still in high school."

"Leigh, no leather." Clearly, Jantzen expected an argument. "Doable?"

Leigh glared at Jantzen, then blew out her cheeks, giving in. "At least I'm good with math. Someone needs to keep track of what Giselle spends. Okay," she called to the rest of the room, "who's got something I can wear?"

Items appeared, several flying through the air her direction, a number of them little better than the leather straps and leggings she preferred.

Joanie called, "Peach Fuzz! All too human. Should go, too."

"What? People out there know me, and I don't do silly very well." Despite his protest, Garik anticipated what he might find. It had been dark when they arrived, but he knew the area where the warehouse was located at Coolidge and Royal. Kang's Garage was a few blocks northwest, and from there, Garik could find his way anywhere in Bay City.

"Jantz," Giselle began to whine.

"Joanie's right. He *is* high school, and he'll make you two more believable. Garik, are you good with that?"

He shrugged. "Sure." Secretly, he was elated. The kids from school would be in class, so he wasn't too worried about being recognized. As long as they stayed away from Old Town where he had lived with his aunt, no harm done.

A new wardrobe for Garik's adventure was assembled from what they could find, some of it from what others had worn in their escape from the Tower. Garik stood in front of the small mirror in the tiny half bath with a black beanie pulled half down over his ears, a black turtleneck from Jantzen, a weathered brown leather jacket, and chunky shoes, Leigh's, he thought. Jantzen had rummaged about for sunglasses to hide his eyes, assuring Garik that the upper half of his face was eighty percent of recognition. The beanie and glasses would hide him from anyone who didn't know him well.

Irina and Arik, Garik imagined, but they would be at the apartment. Everyone else he knew would be at work or at school. He felt reasonably safe.

Giselle and Leigh were into their "silly schoolgirl" act before they stepped outside the door. They had canvassed Julia's things for a supply of gum, and they both popped it continually as they walked. Garik felt his face warm as they pulled the door wide, and the two women hemmed him in and each one took an arm, wrapping theirs in his and immediately fawning over him, touching his shoulders and leaning their heads in against him before pointing to nothing in the distance and giggling.

"Are you serious?" Garik groaned. He'd rather be back in the ring fighting Justin. At least then, he'd known how the match was going to end.

"We're silly schoolgirls," Giselle said, vamping, and she popped her gum.

"Yeah, boyfriend." Leigh grinned, more mocking than infatuated. "Pretend you're having a good time. It's not so hard." She stroked his forearm and pursed her lips into a kiss. She released it his direction and leaned forward to say something to Giselle before laughing like it was funny.

"Supplies," Garik reminded them, knowing better than to try to shake them off. He might as well play along, at least for as long as he could stand it. "Who has the money?"

Giselle pulled out a folded stack of bills from a pocket, and she flashed it with a grin before making it vanish. "Now, this way, or that?" She pointed with a bent wrist south along Coolidge, then north along the same street. South, the building fronts sported furious graffiti, but heading north, the streets became cleaner.

"Kang's Garage is on Meyers." Garik pointed slightly northwest.

Leigh pulled his arm down and waggled her finger in his face, whispering, "Silly, silly boy," with an outsized giggle.

"Okay, don't think I know silly, but that way." He pointed with his head. "Coupla blocks past Meyers is a station with vending machines. I think also one of those glass cases with food inside. That's the closest thing."

They tugged him along that way, stepping off the curb onto Center, then heading toward Summit. There were no stoplights this far south, just four-ways. At Norfleet Street, they paused at their first pedestrian crossing light and waited for the walk sign to grant them passage. Two cars and a delivery truck passed. Neither seemed to pay any attention to the three "teens" absconding from classes at Bay City High.

"Nearly there?" Leigh popped her gum and grinned. "I'm getting tired of silly."

"Columbine and Calloway, and the next one is Cowden. I think the station's on Cowden, a block or two west."

"Left, right?" Giselle giggled at her play on words.

"Oh, girl, you are a funny one." Leigh leaned into Garik, put her hand on his chest, and tapped it twice before straightening up, looking around at the buildings as if taking in something she'd never seen before, and chewing her gum with her mouth open.

Garik hadn't considered, but she probably never had. He wondered who else in the Corona Tower project had never been out in the city. Likely, most of them, if they were part of the human-hybrid experiments.

By Cowden, they were walking down the left side of the street. Garik tried to be light and bright, a high schooler out on the town during the day, skipping classes for a lark, but he'd looked left as they crossed Meyers and had seen the sign for Kang's Garage two blocks down. It wasn't lighted, so he doubted anyone was there, but the alley behind the shop was where he'd hit the jackpot with his Street Strider. It had been a wreck, but it was his, and he'd fixed it up on a thread. Now, it was likely Arik's—or sold so the man could fuel whatever habits kept him away from the apartment more days than not.

At Cowden, the sign for LUCKY! Station flashed to the left but five blocks away. Smaller and just readable, underneath it exclaimed, *Get Your Power on Powerline.*

Giselle muttered, "More time to be found out."

"Yeah, I didn't remember it being that far down." Garik was distracted by the aromas of the city, ones he'd never felt enmesh him so fully, and they throbbed in his senses. Unburnt gasoline from the tailpipes of cars, coffee from an open door, cinnamon rolls somewhere making him hungry. The overwhelming wash of perfume as one woman walked by.

And the sounds. He guessed he'd never paid attention before, not really. Notes in car engines that suggested worn rings, the purr of the expensive models, and stones in the treads of tires that clipped along the pavement in a repetitive pattern. He forced the sounds away, tamping them down until they came out of only one small speaker in the sound system in his head.

He realized he could tune them out if he tried, mostly.

Along Powerline Drive, the fresh hiss of morning traffic percolated like coffee in a kettle. A yellow car hit its brakes, and it ducked out of the flow to pull into the station like cream into coffee. Its brake lights disappeared as the station obscured it.

He caught his reflection in a plate glass window across Cowden, bright against the shadow of the building behind him. The creak of a sign overhead—metal against glass—clawed at his ears. His image twisted in the glass, a nightmare Garik, with his forehead low and his arms past his knees. He jerked his eyes away.

"What? Did you see something?" In the question, Leigh morphed into the fighter the military had hoped to breed into their human-hybrid program, alert and aware. She frowned as she looked around, an indication she was probing the surrounding area. "No one here, boyfriend."

"Except the gorilla in the reflection."

"Gorilla?" Giselle looked at him sharply. "Leigh, you sure no one's following us? If Weston's tracking us, well, we can't take that risk."

"Hey!" Garik laughed roughly, surprised they were

panicking over his silly response to a reflection. "Just a noisy sign and seeing me in the glass. Just there." He nodded across the street, and sure enough, he was still hunched over. He didn't really look that much like a gorilla. He supposed he was spending too much time thinking about Marisa and the images she'd drawn for him that last night together on the roof, Halo Sunchaser attacking a silverback gorilla with her electrified sword. He guessed he would see silverbacks and swords every-where until he was with her again.

Gieselle had her hand on his shoulder, and she leaned against him like a teen girl would intertwine with her first boy crush. She snapped her gum and popped it, grinning. "I didn't hear any noisy sign, but you can be my gorilla anytime, so long's you stay in that window. Here, you be Garik, all-too-human boy, out for the day and skipping school. Yo-kay?" She grinned prettily at him.

"Yo-kay, Mother," he said, but he felt lighter, and he did a little skip with his feet.

"Yeah, Giselle, the boy's gettin' it. Whoo-hoo! LUCKY!'s, here we come."

THE YELLOW car had exchanged places with a white delivery van by the time they reached the station, but the three "teens" thought nothing of it. It was likely filling up at the pumps, though they were on the other side. The tinted windows kept the occupants secreted away, but then who cares who's driving a delivery van?

The cashier gave them little more than a second glance when they entered, but as they browsed the refrigerated food cases, he kept looking at a sheet of paper on the wall, then their direction. As they paid their bill, Garik followed his eyes to the paper.

BE ON THE LOOKOUT—ESCAPEES . . .

Three rows of pictures jostled for space underneath, and he jerked his eyes away, running them along Powerline, searching, his heart pounding.

"Let's go," he hissed, grabbing two sacks and slamming into the door with his shoulder. The cold air hit his face like truth in a field of lies. They weren't teens—well, he was, but not like that—and they weren't skipping school, and they weren't free to wander Bay City.

They were on the run.

He focused on the white delivery van. Was it a real delivery van, or was it a mobile Secret Service covert operation on wheels? Nothing seemed safe. Nothing!

"And that was for?" Leigh had gotten a Twizzlers and she was biting off one end, just as a teen girl would do.

"Didn't you see it? That man was checking to see if we were on that wanted poster."

"Wanted poster?" Giselle giggled and turned. "I want to see."

"No! Have you people never been in the real world?

Do you even know about wanted posters? The Tower can find us because people will turn us in." He felt the panic from his first night in the Tower's basements burning in him. "That van, what if they are in there watching us right now?"

"Not likely." Leigh licked her lips. "These are good. Besides, boyfriend, I watched the driver go into the restroom. He didn't even look my direction. Probably doesn't like high school girls."

"He would if he'd seen me," Giselle teased.

They were to the street, waiting on the light to cross Cowden. Garik felt, no, *heard* something from behind them. He was already turning to look when the back doors of the van opened, and out jumped two men in one-piece drab green coveralls. "Hey, you three," one called.

"How did I miss them?" Leigh turned pale.

"Sorry, we're late for school," Giselle called loudly, while frantically waving a hand and laughing. "We're not skipping, promise." She held up three fingers in a Girl Scout promise. Then she hissed, "Run!"

Run! The same word Garik had called to Marisa that night in the basement of Corona Tower. She had run—and gotten away—and he had been brought down by BolaWraps around his legs.

He didn't want to be brought down again.

To the left—back the way they had come—a military transport paused between two buildings as if searching. To the right was the right-of-way and the Cowden Street Overpass. Garik wondered what had distracted him. He had heard something, should have *known* it was from inside the van. Then the walk light changed, pointing the way, and they took off deeper into the city.

Even the wrong way was better than no way when the bad guys were coming to haul you away.

— 6 —

hey might be on the run, but Garik's heart pounded at the possibility of visiting the skate park only three blocks ahead. It was an interwoven thread to a life that had once been his—and one he wanted back, if he could have it.

The park's convoluted surface consumed the entire block between Connel Street and Forest Avenue and ran from Avenue C (which they were on) north to Avenue B. They could dart in there if they were still being followed. He knew it like the inside of his shoe, and he was already thinking of places they could disappear from view of the street.

Calloway, one block south of Cowden, was one of the few streets that continued west past the grassy right-of-way without a name change, though there was no overpass, and to get from one portion of the street to the other meant hooking north to either Cowden or Avenue C, depending on which side you were on, and taking the Cowden Street Bridge over the right-of-way, then around and back onto Calloway. Calloway to the west continued for seven blocks before making a dead end at Birch.

Between Avenue C and Calloway, a laser strike of an alleyway cut between the buildings and offered service access to the bowels of each business. It also offered protection from prying eyes for three fugitives from the Tower's nefarious human-hybrid DNA recombination program.

Once over the bridge and across Park Avenue, Garik guided them south at Douglas and into the alley, pulling several metal trash cans into the path of anyone that might follow them. Overhead, a powerline rubbed against the brick, swish, swish. Garik looked up, found it, and dismissed it as nothing. Leigh kept reporting what she was finding, but even Garik could see that using her ultrasonic ability distracted her. Once, she nearly tripped over a trash can, and Giselle barely caught her arm before she stumbled. Halfway down the alley, a narrow passage between two buildings gave him a partial view of the skate park. A mother wrapped in a heavy coat and a scarf held a dog on a leash while her son ran around the park bouncing a ball and screaming in joy when it careened over the canted surfaces.

"The skate park's out." Garik sighed. He didn't have a board, but he had such good memories there, and they were almost close enough to touch. Then the white van pulled past, blocking his view of the skate park for a moment, and Garik jerked away from the opening.

"What did you see?" Giselle tried to lean past him, and he put out an arm to block her.

"The van. They might be looking for us." He smelled the odor of its engine, the same as it had been in the parking lot. It was etched in his brain.

"And maybe they just wanted directions, but yeah, maybe they were." Leigh leaned her head against the wall, her face strained.

"Headache, again?" Giselle paused to see if Leigh was okay.

Leigh nodded. "The reason I don't use it often."

"Did you see the military transport?" Giselle questioned Garik. "That's what the Tower would send in."

"Yes." He kept his attention on Leigh. She looked like she was in pain. "How can we help you, Leigh?"

"Someplace quiet for a while. I'll be okay."

"We came north to get here. Can we go south to get back? Then cut across?" Giselle looked upward, perhaps trying to read the city by the way the sky fell against the tops of the buildings.

"If we want to circle the Ransom to get to the Avenue G Bridge. Otherwise, no." Garik had always liked the right-of-way cutting a deep green swathe into the city. Now, it was a barrier that fought them for freedom. "I can get us back."

"Okay," Leigh said, holding one hand over her eyes. "Which direction?"

"West." The direction of The Flower Shop and his aunt's apartment building. He didn't expect to find help in either of those locations, but they were who he was. That connection was stronger than caution or safety.

And besides, Giselle and Leigh didn't seem to know Bay City well. What could a little detour hurt?

Garik's heart pounded as he led the women out of the alley, north to Avenue C, and left towards Sycamore. Just on the other side were the flower-filled shop and the one place in Bay City that had been his home.

All he really wanted was to see the flower shop, to have that small connection with Marisa, just a glimpse of something to remind him of the one girl he'd always loved. He missed her. He missed her more than anything else the Tower had taken from him.

TRAFFIC CRAWLED over the intersections when the lights changed, some with blinkers turning left or right, others offering up flashing brake lights at empty parking spaces. Backup lights flickered on, promising an extended lane blockage and sending oncoming cars into the adjoining lane.

Garik glanced inside several of the cars as the doors opened, revealing the sheen of leather or matte finish of worn cloth, the winter overshoes kicked aside, along in case of snow or rain. He could smell the differences, leather, wood, vinyl, ordinary people, ordinary lives, disappearing into offices or stores to continue their ordinary days.

At one intersection, a car turning right paused to let them pass, sending chills down Garik's back. Like they were evaluating if they had seen him on a missing persons poster. The feeling down his back had him picturing the hackles on a dog or a wolf, and despite himself, he wondered if gorillas had hackles.

Likely not. They were primates. One check for wolf DNA. One X for the gorilla in the reflection.

Garik tried to see the humor in the situation and was derailed when the white van from earlier idled past as they waited at Strickland. People crowded around, and the van didn't stop or seem to notice them. Garik glanced back down Avenue C, concerned about the military vehicle. Search and recovery. Wasn't that what the military was good at? Traffic was heavier—likely because of the hour and being closer to Sycamore—and he couldn't locate it.

At Mayberry—still two blocks away from the

flower shop—Garik caught his first glimpse of the store's sign on the west side of Sycamore. It flickered on, meaning it was nine o'clock. Opening time. Mr. Bruni would unlock the front door, step outside, and set out several containers of the store's brightest blooms, in winter, usually pansies or poinsettias. They were an advertisement to step in and browse for brighter, better blooms.

Garik was so focused on the flower shop that he stepped in front of a turning car, igniting a small windstorm of near calamity. Tires screeched, a horn honked, Giselle yanked his arm.

"Whoa, boy. Didn't you hear that? What's got you distracted?" She smiled and waved at the driver, popping her gum, and circled her ear with one finger. *Looney boy*, she seemed to say. The driver waved and drove on, slowing halfway along the block at an empty parking space.

"Just—" he started to explain, then choked back his words. It was seeing the Bruni's flower shop and remembering the hours he'd spent there with Marisa poking his nose in the cases, smelling the flowers, imagining the ones he'd give her on all the special occasions of her life, if only he had the money to do so. It was his distorted reflection in the plate glass window and Giselle making a thing of it like maybe it was true, he really was a gorilla, and his arms just hadn't grown out yet.

The thought would fry anyone's brain, especially after watching Justin *molt*. Just *shed his skin and come out different*. Well, not completely different. He was still Justin, but he certainly wasn't the *same*.

And his dream during the night. He hadn't been able to shake it off. Rodheimer, with his massive shoulders, saying Garik was *just like him*.

No. He didn't think he could say any of that.

"Just careless." Garik shrugged. "Don't want Leigh to feel like she's the only one with a clumsy foot."

"At least she didn't almost get run over!" Giselle hissed the words, even as she smiled and popped her gum.

Then they were at Sycamore, and the flower shop was just across the road. Garik stood, longing—for what, he didn't know, since Marisa would be at school—when the door began to open, and Marisa stepped into the sunshine, set two plants on either side of the door, hugged her shop smock tighter against the cool air, placed an envelope in the mailbox beside the door, glanced up and down the street, and stepped back inside.

It was like a breath of mountain air and a screwdriver in the gut at the same time. To see her and have her disappear. How could he not go to her, and how could he explain that he'd not been in Russia all this time?

How could he risk her parents' shop, revealing the

secret of the Tower's basements? How could he risk that she might see through the boy he still wanted to be and find the monster the Tower hoped to bring out in him?

"Your eyes," Muhammad had said. "I wouldn't have known you."

Marisa was too important to him. How could he risk that he wasn't the same person, that she wouldn't know him, that she might turn away, say, "You abandoned me. Russia is where you belong," and close the door on him?

None of that mattered, not then, not there. He looked both ways along Sycamore, saw a break in the morning rush, and decided the risk was worth it.

"Peach Fuzz, I see your brain working. What's happening in there?" Giselle had her arm wrapped in his and held him in place.

"I've got to see someone. Wait right here." Garik worked his arm free, darted into the street before they could respond, and ignored their calls to *not do this.*

It was Marisa. How could he not?

LEAPING OVER the curb and onto the sidewalk along Sycamore in front of the store, Garik let his fingers touch the blooms just beside the shop's door, flowers Marisa might have tended, blooms she might have caressed as they opened in the warmth of the store's back room. The sharp aroma of the flowers arrested his attention. He'd never realized they smelled so bright and summery. He leaned into the tinted glass, the reflection of his face, his hair, his hands shading his eyes, the only things he could see.

Of course, Marisa wasn't in the showroom. She would be in the stock room at the back of the building. He would use the familiar rear entrance he always used.

He looked to Giselle and Leigh across Sycamore, and he waved and grinned, skipping and jumping to the corner and down the side of the building along Avenue C to reach the vendor's entrance on Elm. How could he not skip? Marisa was just inside. He was ecstatic, and he wanted to laugh out loud. The air, the city, the sunlight. Seeing Marisa. It was life returned to him, like his time in the Corona Tower basements had never even happened.

Opening the door, he heard the familiar ding, and there she was, her back to him, her hands working dirt into the roots of a plant she was putting into a decorative pot.

"Mr. Bruni's not in today. Leave the shipment on the table by the door. If you need me to sign, I'll be a bit." Marisa, preoccupied, her no-nonsense, ordinary self.

"Mari?" Garik's throat caught, and conflicting emotions welled up inside him. Hearing her, listening to her voice, he was consumed with anticipation and angry at the same time, angry that this had been stolen from him, and there had been nothing he could do.

She turned, her enormous eyes taking him in. A dirt-covered hand pushed back her hair over one ear, leaving a smudge at her temple.

"It's you. They said you were back. I'm sorry, Gari. You shouldn't have come. There was nothing I could do." Her eyes filled up and she returned to her plant.

"I don't understand." Garik pulled his cap from his head, yanked his sunglasses off his face, and walked to her side. "Mari, it's me. I've missed you."

"And me, you." She kept her hands in the dirt, packing the roots carefully. "Do you know how lonely the rooftop is when I'm the only one there?"

"Isn't today school?" An acrid smell—deodorant or sweat—seemed out of place in this world of pleasant smells and quiet, familiar memories and jarred the unexpected question from him. "Why are you not in class? Muhammad and Ibn—"

"Okay." She pushed the partially completed planting back, took a damp towel, and wiped her hands. She sniffled, pressed the towel to her nose, then tossed it into a basket on the floor to join other used towels. "Breaking the law isn't okay, Garik. I'm disappointed in you."

"Breaking the law?" What!? He had done nothing wrong. He had been *kidnapped!*

"We were wrong, Garik, to break into the Tower's basements, and I was sad you were sent back to Russia, but that's the way it is. You can't sneak back into the country illegally."

"I never left. I've been imprisoned in the Tower since that night—"

"That's what they said you would say." She looked behind him, sighed, and pulled a clean towel from a stack, pressing it to her eyes. "My parents, this shop. They haven't let me forget. They will close us down. I had to let them do what they wanted."

"What? What did you let them do?" Garik turned to see a surveillance camera, one that hadn't been there when he was last here. Emblazoned on the side, the Tower's logo mocked him. He heard the door handle turn before he saw it, and from behind him, booted feet rubbed against the hard floor.

Before he could react to the unbelievable betrayal, the back door burst open, and in rushed two fully suited and weaponized warriors. From the front room, the plastic sheeting separated, and a gloved hand closed in a hard fist, calling out to someone Garik couldn't see.

"It's the boy. We're not letting him get away this time."

— 7 —

cyclone of sensations swirled around Garik, shrouding
him in a sandstorm of data.

Sounds battered him, the ding of the overhead bell
attached to the door, slower and lower in tone than he
expected, and more from the front room, the additional
scuffling of feet, someone not yet in his view.

Smells eddied in the air, the adrenalin wash of success coming from the direction of the gloved fist, and
Marisa, regret tinged with something he couldn't
define.

Emotions bared his heart with surprise, anger, the knife thrust of why, why, why. Dismay and disbelief at the precarious situation that had come out of nowhere to yank him back to reality twisted into him, cutting at him. The wind-driven rush of past and present, the purity of what his life had been and the black morass it had become was a hammer shattering his brief hope for happiness.

The Tower was his enemy, and he had no way to fight them, not alone, not without the hybridized humans who had escaped alongside him. Even Marisa . . . *no!* The tide of anger rising inside consumed everything else.

With unprecedented clarity, in a way he had never seen anything before, he envisioned the person attached to the gloved fist—a woman!—in her riot mask, carrying a BolaWrap at her waist with tear gas and a slug-based weapon ready for her use. The person she called to was a man, tall and muscular—how did Garik know that?!—and he was on the radio to a backup team.

The white van. Garik knew it! They were scouts for the military vehicle that had been canvassing the city streets. Within minutes, the flower shop would be swarmed with pursuers. Giselle and Leigh, he had to warn them.

His path out of the mess he'd duped himself into was obvious. He could see it play itself out like it had already happened. Duck, push the small table of flowers aside as he went down, and send the blooms skittering across the floor. The men at the back door would be distracted just enough for Garik to shoulder one in the stomach, kick the other beside one knee, and be out the back door with one of their weapons in his hands.

That wasn't the play he intended to make. He could save himself, but that wouldn't save Giselle and Leigh. That path would place them inside the back of the white van, their hands cuffed and their mouths taped shut. Garik's only option was to exit through the front door.

He brought one leg up, swung it around, and felt his chunky boot impact one man's wrist. He was certain by the sound he left it broken. The man with the broken wrist fell into his companion, disorienting him just enough for Garik to fling himself to the floor, sliding toward the plastic-covered doorway leading into the shop's front room. He glanced at Marisa as he passed, her face still glued to where he used to be, so beautiful, just as he remembered her. *"I had to let them do what they wanted."* How bad had the Tower made life for her that it had come to this? Then she was out of sight and he was in the main room surrounded by the cases of flowers on display. The tall man was just walking through the front entrance, and Garik dove past, smashing into the glass door with his shoulder, and feeling it shatter as he fell into the sunlight. The radio the man held in one hand flew into the air, remaining there, poised in flight. Garik stopped just at the curb. The man still held his hand where the door used to be, unaware for the moment that it was no longer there.

Giselle and Leigh were statues across the street, frozen, waiting, Leigh looking like she was about to yell a warning. The sun cast a strange set of shadows, off in their colors, with refracted rainbows around everything. Even the cars on the street seemed frozen in their little pools of rainbows. Garik felt cold, so cold, as if the day had gone from one season to the next in a matter of moments.

Then he slowed, and the sound of the world around him crashed into him like an ocean wave. Three cars flashed past down Sycamore, their horns blaring at the young man standing nearly in the street. Behind him, the tall man let out a loud exclamation and tumbled outward, carried by the momentum of the door he had been holding. He stumbled and fell, knocking over one of Marisa's pots, and he landed heavily beside Garik. His radio hit the sidewalk beside him, shattering as it landed.

Garik looked down at him, took in the weapon and the BolaWrap at his waist, and a Taser—something the woman inside hadn't carried. Garik felt his new future open up before him. The man was military-trained, and he would recover quickly. He intended to roll over, wrap Garik's ankle in the crook of his arm, and in one singular motion, slam the Taser against Garik's leg. The woman would rush out with her gun extended, see the confrontation, and decide to protect her partner at any cost. She would fire at Garik, but with his quickness and hearing, he would pivot his body to avoid the impact, and the bullet would ricochet off the metal curb edge and impale a car already heading down Sycamore, causing a crash involving multiple vehicles.

A localized disaster that would spread, taking innocent victims in its wake, something Garik could not allow. He yelled across the street, "Run!" and relaxed when the two women only hesitated for a moment before turning and disappearing into the background of the city. They could warn the rest of the team if he could lead their abductors away. The scene that had played itself out in his mind might happen exactly as he had seen it, but he was equally certain he intended to do everything he could to change it.

No one dies today, and he meant it.

The man beside Garik stirred. Garik caught the sound of the woman inside drawing her weapon—even though he couldn't see her!—and he began to move, shifting the world into rainbow shadows once again. Just before the world faded completely away, he heard a voice—Marisa's—calling his name.

By then, it was too late. To those watching, Garik might have blurred and vanished, but to him, silence reigned as his speed ripped at his muscles and consumed his available energy. He collapsed three blocks down Sycamore, having made it into the park-like grounds surrounding the Old City Hall. Fire consumed him, his muscles cramping all over his body, and he could barely catch his breath.

He wondered if this was how Jantzen felt each time he evaporated into purple fog.

Before he could come up with an answer, tires screeched from back the way he had come, metal tore into metal, and with an explosive concussion, black smoke boiled into the sky.

Maybe, Garik thought, this was why Christian didn't fight what he knew was about to happen. If he tried to avoid it, something worse took its place.

Then sirens flooded the sky, and all Garik could do was say a prayer that everyone involved was all right. Around him, tables were set up for an event, with chairs, a speaker's platform, and bunting. Sodas sat atop a red ice chest under a sign proclaiming Bay City Fitness Run. Already people were gathering, several in fitness gear stomping their feet to stay warm. He couldn't stay here. He had to get to safety—and back to help the others, if he could.

He stood, his body fighting him in electrified jerks and uncoordinated twitches. And he *hurt!* He hoped this wasn't his future as a hybridized human. He watched two military-style vehicles roar south, likely heading from Corona Tower along Sycamore to either the crash or the incident at The Flower Shop. The street curved just enough that they were out of sight before they slowed.

He hoped—*he wanted!*—Marisa to be okay. He had to know. He lifted one arm to find his black cap still clenched in his fist. His sunglasses were lost, but he slipped the cap over his head, forced himself to concentrate on his coordination, and worked his way through the paths wending through the Old City Hall grounds before heading west on First. By the time he reached Oak, he could walk normally, though he wasn't sure he could run again if he wanted. His mind, his cunning, his planning would have to be his path to survival. Whatever he had done at the Bruni's store was like being jerked through a worm hole—deadly to everyone involved.

He veered south on Elm, and crossing Avenue B, he began working his way from storefront to storefront. The flower store was only a block away, and about halfway down the row of businesses, he had a partial view of both the north entrance that faced Avenue C and the vendor's entrance on Elm.

Old Town started west of Sycamore, and several of the buildings Garik moved along exposed vacant painted-over windows. For Rent signs had become the blood of Old Town bleeding out. The lack of traffic left Garik feeling exposed. Without his sunglasses, he was certain every person in Bay City knew exactly where he was. The "afterglow" of running at top speed had him convinced not to try that again.

His connection with Marisa assured him it was worth whatever it cost.

Garik adjusted his position for a better view and located two military vehicles parked along Avenue C. One had two doors open, and several people in camo kept glancing left and right. Garik sank into a doorway, hoping to become part of the scenery. The door to the shop opened, and he involuntarily tried to disappear.

"It was what you wanted."

Garik's ears perked up. Marisa! He warmed to her voice and tried to see her, but he was blocked by a group of signs on the corner of Elm and Avenue C.

"I didn't warn him or sabotage anything. Check your video."

"He's gone, isn't he?" The woman's voice with the fist. "We had our best here. How could he know—"

"How should I know? You people are in control, at least that's what you say. You made me the bait, and he got away, and now it's my fault?"

"Don't forget, young lady. Your parents' business is only operational as long as we allow it to be. Work with us. We're warning you."

"If he *were* in Russia, how could he have gotten back into the country so easily—"

"Just do as you're told. If he comes back again, we want to know."

The voices stopped, the vehicle doors slammed, and with a roar, they pulled away. They turned north on

Elm, drove right past him, and their brakes flashed at Avenue B and Avenue A before turning east on First. Overhead, a powerline swayed in the wind, rubbing insulation to insulation. The sound came to him as a whisper, suggesting, "There are things you still don't know, wolf boy. Be careful, be careful, be careful." A bird landed, one of the few Garik had seen in, well, since forever. There weren't any birds in the Tower's expansive basements.

Somewhere in the distance, he picked up the activity resulting from the car crash. A firetruck had arrived, and one of the cars was being dismembered to get at what or who was inside.

Garik looked toward the shop, leaning forward enough to see the door, now closed, with Marisa still inside. He had no way of knowing if everyone had left, but it made sense that they had. Likely, the wreck was welcomed, a distraction from the devastation they were deploying on Marisa and her family.

Was that why Mr. Bruni wasn't at the shop? Why Marisa was missing school today? They told her to be the only one there just in case he came to find her? Garik's face burned with the injustice of it all. They had no *right* to do that to her and her family.

He touched his wrist, wishing for his watch. Being back in the city reminded him of how useful it was, to just call, ask how people were doing, what was going on. If he could call John, let them know where he was, find out if they were still safe in the converted warehouse ... then, the Tower could likely trace his call. Pinpoint his location. Send their goons to chase him down, and he didn't think he would get away this time.

Movement at the shop focused him back to his surroundings. The door on Avenue C now boasted a closed sign. Marisa stepped from the back door, her coat wrapped around her slender frame, and she pressed a key into the lock. She lifted her sunglasses and wiped her eyes—*his sunglasses!* She was wearing the ones he had taken off and forgotten.

He wanted to step out and call to her. "I'm here, Mari! I didn't leave. I would never leave. Don't go!"

Yet, *"Your parents' business is only operational as long as we allow it to be."* And Marisa's words. *"You shouldn't have come."*

He had to, he wanted to say. He couldn't have stayed away if he'd wanted. Yet, when he stepped forward to tell her, she was already gone, and despite his despair, he knew his choices weren't his own.

He needed to get back to the warehouse. He needed to know that everyone he'd helped escape was warned.

He had to step up and be what the situation required him to be, even if he had no clear idea exactly what that was.

$$— 8 —$$

arik drew in a deep lungful of air, taking time to winnow the smells into things he must deal with immediately, those that were merely interesting, and others that made up the background of the moment and could be set aside.

The city had never smelled so alive before, so vital, so filled with life. The sterile exhaust of a window air conditioner just across the street. It was likely pumping heat into an office. Something delicious from a block over, possibly streaming from a partially open car window, eggs-and-fries-to-go from Chow Down, an aroma Garik would recognize anywhere.

He also caught the acrid exhaust of the white van, revealing that it had driven down Elm, although not since he'd set foot on the street. Fainter, the rotting odor of something dead, likely a rat in the sewer or a trash bin from the alley behind him.

Teasing him, a wafting cloud of odor called, "Here's something interesting. Explore me," and Garik's attention was pulled to the corner to see a red-attired pizza delivery girl appear on a moped with a stack of pizzas strapped behind her.

Entombed within the smell were the burned odor of the oil in the engine, the leather polish she'd used on her shoes that morning, and her shampoo, something with coconut in it.

No judgement, just information, and he soaked it all in. He tried to find Marisa in the inrush of data, but she had been outside and gone, and inside the flower shop, the blooms and the gloved woman had added so many layers of smells that he hadn't had time to sort them into their respective slots in his brain.

Now, the burning of hydrocarbons drifted over the buildings, mixed with the organic proteins of fire-fighting foam. Fear drifted in and out, sharp and acrid, the thorny prick of pheromones released by people possibly injured. The aromatic wash of flour and cheese and oregano from the pizza girl had begun to fade, and he realized how hungry he was. What had happened to the bag of food he had carried? Somewhere in the flower shop, he figured—gone—and he had no money to buy more.

Aunt Irina? City View Apartments was three blocks west. Surely she would be glad to feed him. The possibility flashed in front him, a lightbulb of hope, and was as quickly dismissed. He didn't know the day of the month, and her kitchen cabinets might be as sparse as the businesses around him displaying open signs.

St. Anne's, his church of choice, maintained a food pantry, but it was located on Spruce, twelve blocks away. Every block he walked the streets—or even the alleyways—was another chance to be discovered by the Tower. A shift in the wind returned the smell of flour, cheese, and oregano, and he pictured the girl on the moped. Old City Hall. The Fitness Run. He caught an announcement over a loudspeaker filtering between the buildings welcoming participants to the day's events. The pizzas would be out on the tables, runners standing around chatting, a mixture of faces from across the city. Black, white, brown, and an amalgam of everything in between. Did he dare try to blend in, even for pizza?

He was starving. He pulled his knit cap down, worked it over his ears, and kept his head low. Turning east on Avenue A brought him to the south side of the Old City Hall. Cars lined the sidewalks. People were still gathering, most in some sort of running gear, with brightly colored shoes, snug pants, and bulky layers from the waist up. Knit caps dominated the headwear—thank goodness—and Garik fell in with a pride of runners in puffy winter coats. They broke off to collect their identification lanyards, and he continued to the food table where he could see the pizzas stacked in their boxes. Paper plates and napkins were laid out, ready to use.

"Too cold for you today?"

Garik looked up from the pizzas to discover a petite woman in a thick coat and gloves. Earmuffs buried her ears amidst a cloud of blonde hair.

"A little," he said, hoping she didn't expect him to carry on a conversation.

"For me, too. I usually participate to prepare for the Bay City Marathon—my daughter, Regina, attends Bay City High, and I can't let her show me up—but the forecast was for a chilly day, so I volunteered to oversee the food tables. I can train for the marathon another time." She laughed like it was an inside joke. "Can I get you a slice of pizza to warm you up? Observers are certainly welcome to enjoy the food. We have another delivery coming at noon, and this won't stay warm for long."

"Yes, please." He watched hungrily as she opened the top box, showed him hamburger for his permission, and handed him a slice when he nodded. "Thank you."

"We have drinks if you want one," she offered.

He nodded and bit in, inhaling the pizza as quickly as he could chew. She already had a second slice ready, laughing that he was already done. Others were wandering over, and when she began to lay out pizza for them, Garik stepped to the next table for a can of soda. He popped the tab and worked his way under a tree to hide himself as much as possible. Regina, he thought. The lady must be Mrs. Kournikova, Regina Kournikova's mother. He had recognized Regina in the woman's eyes, and when she had handed him the pizza, he smelled cherry blossoms. Regina had once said her mother liked cherry blossom air freshener.

He tried to think if he had ever smelled cherry blossoms on Regina, but being out of circulation since summer defeated that line of mental investigation, and he let it go. He had other things to think about: Marisa; the group who had escaped with him from the Tower; and how to stay out of the Tower's clutches. He was working on that, but it was beyond him at the moment.

He popped the final bite of crust in his mouth, the buttery, salty, yeasty flavor filling up his brain. He had no idea pizza could smell so good—and taste even better. How had he missed that all his years?

He visited the trash receptacle to toss his things, wiping his hands thoroughly before dropping them in. Before he could step away, Regina's mother joined him to deposit several empty plates.

"The award ceremony is at two. Good luck to you

and yours. Maybe I will see you there."

"Thank you, Mrs. Kournikova."

"You must be one of Regina's friends. Be sure to check our giveaway table. It's all branded, but free sunglasses!" She laughed. "I see you didn't bring any."

"I will. I appreciate the offer."

"Corona Tower's offer. They sponsor us." She handed him a water bottle. The side said, Bay City Fitness Run, and underneath was the Corona Tower logo.

Garik smiled, took the bottle, and tucked it into a pocket. At the giveaway table, he selected the least garish glasses—black frames with Bay City Fitness Run in neon pink down the earpieces—and a bottle band that he could hook over his water bottle and to his belt. He slipped the bottle band in the pocket with the water bottle to put on later.

He also picked up a map of the Fitness Run course and was relieved that it stayed on the West Side, following Second west to The Cliffs, then north before twisting through the Shady Ridge Acres residential area, then on to circle Waldorf's before weaving east to Birch and south along Birch to the finish line back at the Old City Hall. Several shorter routes were marked for different age groups or fitness levels. The run along Birch would be uphill, and being at the end of the run, it would likely defeat all but those in the best shape.

Now that he had pizza in his stomach, Garik

considered the people he had seen prepping for the run. He could beat them all, and the competitor in him wanted to shed his coat and toss off the full run. It would be a breeze for him, but it would also draw attention to his presence out and about in the city. He sighed, returned the map to the table, set his new sunglasses on his face, and pressed the button to trigger the light across Sycamore. The breeze coming off the bay carried fish and seaweed and diesel, stronger than he previously remembered. He also smelled Chow Down, the eatery at the Corona Mall, reminding him of his fugitive status.

He pulled his knit lower on his face, and when the light changed, he made his way across, walking as casually as he could to try to blend in.

GARIK HAD passed the cross-tipped spire of First United Congregation three blocks to the north on Thomas and the Bay City Transportation Department two blocks later, also to the north and bordered by McKinley, Second, Douglas, and Third, when he noticed the buzzing sound of a drone navigating the streets in a grid-like pattern.

He backed under an awning between Douglas and Eisenhower, hunching his shoulders in his leather jacket, even as he was aware it didn't make him less prominent against the gray of the concrete sweeping him along towards the First Street and Powerline overpass.

"If only I had my Street Strider," he muttered. Riding the jet-assisted bike would hardly be less obvious, but faster was the key, and it would bring less attention than running full out. Running, people would think him a thief or some other hooligan-type character, and they would report him for sure.

He checked his knit cap, ensured it covered as much of him as possible, secured his new Fitness Run glasses on his face, and listened over the low rumble of background noise—the lifeblood of the city—for the drone. The overpass was two blocks away with a light he had to navigate at Park on the near side and another at Powerline once he crossed. He could see the sign for Kerre's Dive at Garfield and First. If he could reach there, he could navigate south and bypass the gridwork of lighted crosswalks through alleys and courtyards.

A second drone caught his attention, this time creating a high-fidelity symphony of stereophonic dread. The music crashed in his ears, turning his stomach over, while assuring him his window of safety was about to end in a cymbal clash of reverberating disaster. He watched the intersection at Park, judging the timing of the walk light. Giving himself half a minute before it changed, he stepped from under the awning and strode confidently toward his destination.

The whine of the drones changed. Garik cringed and walked faster. They both screamed at him from directly overhead, and he began to run. Forget the lights. He was going across.

Events reached a crescendo when the roar of approaching military vehicles began to reverberate against the walls of the concrete canyons.

"No, no, no," Garik breathed, muttered, and prayed, all at the same time. The sun flashed against his face as he crossed the bridge, hot on his skin, leaving the morning chill to prickle any part of him in shadow. The winter-dead grass along the right-of-way filled the air with a dusty and wasted chlorophyll fog, an acrid aroma trapped in the grassy wasteland and escaping into the air directly above.

Escape. Garik reached the far side of the bridge, desperate. He dodged a delivery truck emblazoned with the name and logo for Howie's Hoagies and aimed for the drive-thru portico at Kerre's Dive.

He would have made it, he was certain. He almost did. Then, the sound of the drones grew sharp and angry. He heard tires skidding to a stop and voices began to yell. Then, his body was hit, and he knew exactly what it was.

A BolaWrap encircled him, its octopus arms wrapping his torso, his legs, and his upper limbs in a loving embrace. On the way down, his Fitness Run sunglasses flew from his face, and the brilliance of the sun blinded him for a moment.

"Two pairs of sunglasses in one day," was his last

thought as he hit the concrete. With a jarring impact, the sun went out, and night was all he could see.

GARIK CAME to strapped to a gurney, his eyes blurry. He rocked back and forth in a medical transport. A white-suited technician talked into a laptop.

Weston Rodheimer was on the other side.

"Just the boy, then?" Rodheimer filled the screen, his heavy brows and jaw sitting on his too-broad shoulders.

"We were lucky the mother recognized this one. Otherwise, we would have missed him, too. She only remembered his face when he called her by name."

The mother. *Mrs. Kournikova.* Garik wanted to pound himself in the head. If only he hadn't said her name.

"No luck involved. He planned this. Bring him in."

Planned this? Who, him? That was a laugh. Then the computer screen began to blur, Rodheimer faded away, and the technician, well, Garik hadn't seen his face and wouldn't mind if he never did.

Somewhere, he thought he might have pleaded, "This time, please don't cut my hair."

Before he could decide if he had only thought the words, darkness overtook him a second time, stealing even that from him.

— 9 —

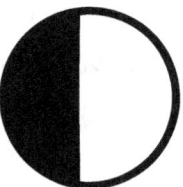

utside the big window, snow had started to fall.

Bay City was like a lightly frosted cake, pretty, or it would be if Garik wasn't seeing it from atop the Corona Tower in the penthouse suite.

His image shimmered faintly in the heavily tinted glass, revealing his outline crowned by bushy hair— *they hadn't cut it!*—and the whites in his eyes that seemed crisper than he'd ever seen them.

Was that what Muhammad had meant, he wondered? Or maybe the difference was in the broadness of his shoulders or the thickness of his legs. He adjusted his position slightly, searching for differences in his reflection. He still felt like Garik, but he was also pretty sure Justin still felt like Justin, even if his molting had changed him into something almost unrecognizable.

Would Garik recognize the differences when they happened? Or would he look at his reflection and see what he wanted to see, a high school senior, a were-wolf, *no matter how humanoid*, or, and this continued to play with his mind, a lumbering gorilla with a meaty fist that could smash through tables and walls?

The nightmare hadn't gone away, and after all, Christian with his wolfhound DNA had acquired pre-cognition, and Garik hadn't experienced a moment of that, well, except for those few seconds in The Flower Shop, sensing that there were two attackers in the front room, not just one. He admitted that he might have deduced that through his hearing. None of them had been exactly stealthy in their actions.

He certainly hadn't seen the BolaWrap that had taken him down. If he had, he'd have run the other direction.

Behind him, Weston Rodheimer cleared his throat. It vibrated the floor in a low-pitched rumble, almost a growl.

"I'm almost through," Garik called. Almost through being patient. Almost through with what you've done to me. Almost through with answering your questions, with trying to regain my freedom, with having my girl-friend harassed by your Tower goons.

Outside, it was growing dark in the late fall evening. In the distance, the Ransom Communications Building glowed, and left, he found Bay City Medical and the entrance to the industrial park. His friends were right there, in the warehouse Dieter's father had converted into a skate park, that was if they hadn't been compromised by his clumsy efforts to reconnect with Marisa.

Would Justin be in the air searching for him? Would Garik see him if he were? And how would he signal to him that he was in the Tower and behind the glass on the top floor? Or was he lost once again, with all his Houdini loopholes now sealed away forever?

He looked past his reflection to the room around him mirrored in the glass, everything sharpening up with the darkening sky. Rodheimer reclined in a chair that two people would be comfortable in at a desk nearly as spacious as Garik's bedroom back in Irina's apartment, waiting on Garik to give him the answer he wanted to hear. A fireplace filled with crackling flames warded off the perception of cold through the sealed glass windows.

Garik tightened up one arm, flexing without seeming to flex, comparing his biceps to Rodheimer's and struggling to find the similarities between them. Rodheimer wasn't even flexing, and his arms were still twice the size, and Garik had been working out for months. Sheesh! There was no way he could win against this guy.

Not physically, anyway, but there were other ways to win against a bully, and Rodheimer was that, no denials possible.

Sighing, he turned. "Why should I believe you?"

"Why would I lie to you?" Rodheimer's deep voice rumbled, and Garik thought he caught the images in the glass trembling in respect.

"The same reason you have all along, I don't know. You enjoy kidnapping teenagers and shooting them up with monkey DNA—"

"Timber wolf." Rodheimer almost smiled. "That was a personal choice of mine. I hoped to appeal to a wild city boy like you. And how have you suffered? How are you worse off than before?"

"No freedom." No friends. His girlfriend lied to. And his aunt, what had they told her? Had they gone all the way to Russia to tell his parents his airplane had crashed on the way? If Irina contacted them, they might tell her that their precious son had never arrived. What about that, Director Rodheimer?

"That." Rodheimer stood, becoming bigger than it was possible for any man to be as he rose from his chair. He shrugged. "Our people beg to come for our treatments. How could I know you would be the one person to not appreciate all we could give you? My apologies. Come. Sit in front of the fire."

The big man stepped easily towards the fire, shifted two wingbacks to face it, leaving a small marble-topped table in between. He motioned to Garik to take one of the chairs.

The chair swallowed the teen. He sat up as straight as possible, his feet barely touching the floor. Next to him, Rodheimer filled the chair perfectly, as if it were designed for him. Garik realized it probably was.

"This." Rodheimer opened a drawer in the table and lifted out the black sunglasses from the Fitness Run. "Brilliant, all of it. Jantzen couldn't have done better."

"At what?" Getting caught? he wanted to ask, because Jantzen had been helping him *not* to do that very thing.

"Come now. Modesty is not your friend, not with me. The glasses thing." Rodheimer held up the glasses and looked at the words scrawled down the earpiece. "Quite a clue, and telling that mother her name. Perfect. Planning I didn't expect from you. Rid the compound of your competition, and you would excel."

"Rid the—" Garik clamped down on his response. Did this man actually think he'd let himself be captured on purpose? Even be BolaWrapped, just to abandon his friends without them suspecting? Sheesh!

"I like the way you think. Using your old girlfriend to ditch your two guards . . . bet that caught them by surprise. Good disguise by the way. Without these glasses, my team wouldn't have known it was you. Whoever sorted that out for you is to be commended. Wouldn't surprise me if Jantzen had a hand in it. He always said the eyes are a person's most recognizable feature. Hide the eyes and you hide the person. The reason he wears black beanies. Like the one you wore."

"Yeah, he said that to me, too." Garik sank into his chair, deflated. He'd pictured the Director as a mental goof, the Hulk in a gorilla suit. Now it seemed he had a brain, too.

"So, back in the fold, more like me than you may want to admit." Rodheimer grinned. "My own special additive to your new DNA serum—"

"What?" Garik interrupted. "You said timber—"

"Ha! You amuse me. Like the son I never had. You are third generation. Has Jantzen told you that? Or did he continue to string you along, give you tidbits of lies, just enough to gain your confidence? Well?"

Garik sat, stunned at the words. That was exactly how he'd felt at times, the dark-haired man befriending him, then stepping back as though Garik were an experiment to be evaluated, used if possible, and—he had never dared think it—discarded if he failed to live up to the man's expectations.

"How am I third . . . . your own special DNA . . . I'm confused." Like a salmon fighting a fish ladder and not making good progress.

"See? I do know Jantzen, and very well. He has

shared what he wants you to know. I will tell you the truth." Rodheimer offered Garik the glasses, and he shook his head. The big man placed them in the table and closed the drawer. "If you ever want them, a memento of sorts. I am first generation. We had to start somewhere, and I knew it must be me. Jantzen, also, first generation. You've seen the smoke thing? Of course, you have." Rodheimer lifted his hand, and out of nowhere, a man appeared with a tray of drinks and a large cigar. He held it out to Garik after Rodheimer took a glass of amber liquid.

"These are all . . . alcohol. I'm only seventeen. At least I think. I'm not sure of the date."

"November, late. So, still seventeen. Take what you like. Now that you are, um, modified, your body will slough off all attempts to doctor it with stimulants or depressants. It's a shame, but I like the taste."

Rodheimer threw back one glass, and after Garik took a glass of darker liquid, the servant offered Rodheimer another. He set his second on the table and motioned the man away. Garik sipped the liquid and choked as it burned down his throat.

Rodheimer held out the cigar, admiring it. "This, too, is useless, but I enjoy holding it. Not to light, but just to hold, mind you. Now, to business. That fight with Justin. I watched how you moved. Like you knew where he would be before he knew. Tell me how you did that."

"I, um—" This was a time to choose his words carefully. *Don't reveal everything.* Jantzen had taught him that, and whether the man turned out to be on his side or not, he considered it good advice. "Jantzen had fought him earlier. I watched and copied his technique."

"Copied his technique. Okay, let me tell you what it means to be first generation. We must work harder at keeping our human genes dominate. It doesn't work for all of us."

"Christian."

Rodheimer raised his eyebrows. "Yes, Christian was one. Jantzen and his ability to morph into blue smoke is another. Let me show you something." He held the cigar in his left hand, brought his right to the end, and snapped his fingers. Electricity leaped from his fingertips to the end of the cigar *and stayed there.* The big man bit off the end of the cigar, sucked on it, and it flared into life. He moved his hand away, and when he spread his fingers, the electricity evaporated into the air, leaving a smell of ozone.

"What has DNA like that? Electric eel?"

"Ha, ha! You are the first to suggest that. No, just a side effect, unexpected. You could say I've had the DNA of an electric current melded with my DNA, along with other stuff, and now, this is something I can do. It isn't always pleasurable. My clothing? Specially designed to reduce static charge. My body absorbs it, and I can release it at will. Accidentally at times, which can be deadly to other people."

"I bet. If I'm third generation, how am I different?" That was what Garik wanted to know. What would happen to him when he molted, if that was what happened to him? Would he have Rodheimer's giant shoulders, Justin's extra joints and wings, or would he become a lemur-like person like Marco?

Was it his lot to become a werewolf? He used to love werewolf movies. Now, he couldn't keep them out of his dreams. That and crazy gorillas about to be decapitated with an electrified sword, thanks, Marisa.

"We are striving for balance, bonus capabilities, but not so many that we lose the human connection. To be able to jump long distances, but with recognizably human legs. To think faster, evaluate quicker, but retain a normal cranium size. To develop extended smell but not a rat-like face shape."

"You want us to be like secret agents."

"Exactly!" Rodheimer's level of excitement said he was extraordinarily pleased with Garik's evaluation. "If you become the success we hope to create in you, then your success is everyone's success. You choosing to return to us of your own volition, and so creatively, tells me we are on the right track."

"What about the extraordinary things the people I've trained with can do? Aren't those things useful, also?" Alyna with her razor claws. Julia, able to sense heat with her infrared ability. Laura, able to breathe out hydrogen cyanide, even though Garik had never seen her use the skill, and more . . . Marco, Justin, Leigh, Amy, able to track a hundred enemies at once. Even Paulo, with his fingers able to shoot boiling water. How useful must that be in certain circumstances, and Garik had watched John cool water nearly to freezing just by inserting his hands.

Garik was useless in comparison, and in fact had been less than useless, even a hindrance. Breaking the van window. Nearly getting Leigh and Laura captured. Now, here he was in the Tower *with the big bad guy himself.* Trapped once again, and this time, he was certain they intended to throw away the passkey.

"In context, but not in the general world. If your enemy can see your offensive weapons, they can combat them. If you, however, come to them as a teenage boy, they will welcome you inside, and when you gain their confidence, wham! They are at our mercy!"

Rodheimer slammed his hand down on the table to emphasize the word *wham,* and the marble top cracked in two, leaving the legs canted sideways. Garik reached for the glasses, the room creating rainbow swirls around everything for that singular instance, and he held them in his hands with no spillage at all.

"That's it, boy. You just did it again. Just what I wanted to see. You and me, just alike. Do you see it?"

Garik grinned weakly. What had he done now?

— 10 —

hey were soon aboard the elevator and headed to the basement levels.

Rodheimer inserted his passkey, and the unit prompted him for a palm scan. The panel became a Christmas tree, with options from the 40th floor down to Level 5 in the basement. The mall. That's the one Garik wanted to reach out and touch, but such wasn't to be the case. The big man tapped Basement Level 4.

"That's the hospital." Garik grimaced. Still saying the obvious. Like a kid.

"Correct." Rodheimer watched the display as it flashed numbers almost too quickly to follow.

"I don't have a cold." Making light of it might earn him some information. "Unless you think I brought the outside pandemic in, you know, the one that gives everyone else the urge to try their hand at getting out into the real world."

"Which is why we're headed to Level 4. We intend to lock that possibility away for good."

The final light flashed, the door dinged, and it swung wide. The corridor was a ribbon of candy, with blue stripes along each edge. The air, clean, with no odor of its own, not really, giving it a distinctive aroma that was unique even in the research center.

Scrubbed, purified, and likely kept separate from the air pumping in and out of the other basement levels. No diseases in. No diseases out. What every good hospital should strive for.

Garik was surprised not to see Nurse Ratchett waiting for them at the door. The woman had been pleasant enough, but it was clear that she enjoyed the process better than she enjoyed the people. If you wanted to be a cooperative patient and get your DNA modified to a dragonfly, a woolly mammoth, or whatever, that was perfectly okay to her. Suggest that something else is in your plans, and she'd as soon slap you with her needle, regardless.

"I expected someone to meet us." Garik waited on

Rodheimer before exiting. The man seemed to be making a point with his silence.

"I asked them to clear the floor. Shall we?" Rodheimer moved forward, a ghost walker inside that massive body of his.

Garik understood. Rodheimer had established their relative hierarchy in the Tower. The Director had the power to order everyone off the hospital floor, and Garik had none at all, not even the power to push the elevator button to choose their destination.

Halfway down the corridor, a utility door to the right opened a short distance in front of them. The latch clicked, metal on metal, thump thump, and the door opened a few inches and clicked shut again, echoing hollowly in the unadorned corridor. Rodheimer paused, his eyes hardening, and his forehead becoming a trough of irritation. The door clicked again, and a man backed out, blocking their way, while pulling a wheeled bucket with a mop handle that chattered along every surface it could reach like a wooden drumstick.

Garik recognized Tyrone Brown with his wide smile and white teeth. He and his boss, Joseph Howard, had installed the charger for Garik's ZBoard, the electric skateboard he had used to get around when he and Jantzen had prowled the vast corridors in the 64-square-block underground research facility.

"Mr. Brown." Rodheimer rumbled the man's name, and Tyrone looked around and turned pale, or as pale as his coffee skin could.

"My apologies, Mr. Rodheimer. So sorry." Tyrone tried to catch the door before it closed behind him, and his hand slipped, and it clicked shut. He fumbled out his passkey and dropped it. He stared at it as though devastated by its betrayal.

"Pick it up, Mr. Brown."

The maintenance man did, carefully, and reinserted it into the door, releasing the lock, thump thump. Swinging the door past, he banged the bucket, sloshing water onto the floor. By then, he was visibly shattered.

Garik blanched at the interplay. The Director had played nice up in the penthouse *clearly wanting something Garik had to offer.* There was nothing he wanted or needed from Tyrone, so there was no reason for him to be kind.

Rodheimer's words were a jackhammer in Garik's head. *"We intend to lock that possibility away for good."* How did he plan that? How did the Tower's research program de-Houdini its participants? Leg bracelets? Handcuffs chained to the wall? Tracking devices inserted in the brain that couldn't be removed?

The Nazis had tattooed the prisoners in their gulag system so they could be tracked if they ever escaped. Was that what Garik could expect, a bar code on his forehead that could be read by lasers in every doorway he stepped through? These people could already fiddle with people's DNA. There was no telling what else they could pull off.

Only when Tyrone had disappeared back into the darkness of wherever the door led, Rodheimer cleared his throat and continued walking. At a door marked Experimental Hybridization, he inserted his passkey and stood back, waiting on Garik to enter before following him inside.

At least it didn't say Tattoo Parlor. Garik didn't know if that was better or not. Experimental didn't sound so good.

Inside offered a small anteroom with a desk and more doors just behind. A cage to capture the unwary. Once you get in, you are trapped with no way out except deeper into the dream. A lobster cage, or a psychedelic rabbit hole, falling deeper and deeper as things get weirder and weirder. Garik looked around for signs of magic mushrooms and only saw the candy stripes still hugging the floor. No Alice, not yet.

He wished he'd studied more on Harry Houdini's techniques at escaping in every possible situation. He could use a little escape magic just about now.

A woman stepped through a private door behind the desk, with large earrings and stringy blonde hair.

"My apologies, Director. We're got a situation in experimental surgery and cleanup hasn't arrived."

Her nametag on her smock said Kim. She popped her gum twice before pulling out the chair and sitting down. She was so thin she seemed to disappear into the chair's fabric. She set a computer keyboard on her desk and typed in a query before looking up and smiling.

"All ready, Director."

"Thank you, Ms. Sanchez."

Kim reached under her desk, did something to trigger the second set of doors, and they began to open, releasing a cacophony of tympanic noises that could have raised the dead.

Garik wished for clean underwear. He was certain he would need them before the night was over.

"MEET CHAD."

Rodheimer towered over a disfigured man on an operating gurney. He was in a hospital gown covered with a sheet from the chest down. To the side was a motorized wheelchair. Noises of whining saws and metallic banging filled the background. The room to the door closed, and the sounds muted.

"How are you doing today, Chad? Any fresh escape attempts lately? How are those legs working? Too bad you couldn't keep your originals, but these will be so much better, and they will allow us to see if it is really possible to transpose adaptations from one participant to another."

Chad, from the cafeteria. Garik remembered him. Keep his original legs? Fresh escape attempts? He was cold with the implications.

"Garik, this is Chad Sherwin. You may have seen

him around. We've provided him top-notch transportation, an Invacare Storm Series chair. High torque and brushless motors. Top notch. Chad is very appreciative of our kindness and willingness to provide him the very best. Isn't that so, Chad?"

Chad rolled his eyes. One eye tracked differently, and Chad moved his lips as though answering, but Garik heard nothing.

"I'm sorry, Chad? A little lower, perhaps?" Rodheimer leaned down, putting one ear closer to Chad's face. Chad screwed his face up and closed his eyes, refusing to respond.

"I almost met you once, Chad." Garik took the initiative to ease the situation. "You were with someone named Heath. I was with Jantzen."

Chad pointed to a side table and a small device. Garik handed it to him, and he pressed a switch. When he opened his mouth to speak, the device spoke for him.

"Yes, in the cafeteria several months ago. Your hair looks better now." He smiled, a crooked expression in his lumpy face.

"You have bat DNA, don't you?" It was the only answer. The voice he couldn't hear, the box to speak for him. The unusual facial bone structure. "Your skill is echolocation. I bet you're great to have around in the dark."

"Hear that, Director?" The box spoke, and Chad glared at Rodheimer. "I'm great to have around in the dark."

"Maybe if our little experiment pans out." Rod-heimer grasped one of Chad's legs with a massive hand and squeezed it. Chad grimaced but didn't respond.

"Why are we here?" Again, the question was to diffuse an uncomfortable situation. Garik wanted this over with.

"Ah, back to that. We are having a lesson in what happens to people who are not satisfied with our program and our accommodations." Through the door, the sound of someone screaming brought a sigh from the Director. He looked at the door and waited on it to stop. "How is your back, Chad? I'm sorry your bone structure doesn't allow you to sit erect. If we get your leg bones functioning, maybe you can walk where you need to go. With a torso brace, of course."

"I don't understand." Legs, bone structure, the man's back. Put it together for me, Garik pleaded.

"Bat." Chad's box speaking. "I'm designed to fly, sleep upside down, use my wings like arms. My echolocation is unaffected, but the good Director decided to remove my ability to fly, and now I'm restricted to that." His eyes locked on the chair.

"It was too bad, Chad, but necessary. Your adaptations are invaluable for research, and we can't let them get away. The prosthetic arms, though, seem to function well. And your leg donor was glad to gift them to you. He had no use, otherwise."

No other use for the legs—or for him? Basement Level 5, Garik remembered. Christian, sent there to be recycled into whatever useful parts he could supply.

The door opened, allowing the whine of an electric drill inside. Kim Sanchez leaned in. "My apologies for the noise, Director. We're fitting new prosthetics for several people today, and it can't be helped. Ms. Sunchaser is on the line. Do you wish to speak with her?"

"Wait here." He bored his eyes into Garik, and as he left, the door snapped shut with a metallic click and the thump thump of the locks that trapped them inside.

"IS IT TRUE?" Chad's box asked the evenly modulated question as the man's unusual mouth moved silently.

"I don't know. What?" Garik was searching the room for options to Houdini out of there, even if he did realize they were on the fourth basement level. Still, he had gotten out once. He could do it again.

"You're not escaping a second time."

"What makes you say that?" Garik hadn't said anything about escape although it was everywhere in his mind.

"I escaped. They brought me back. Now look at me. Half of who I was. The Director won't hesitate to do the same to you. You don't seem to have anything to take away, so they will likely add to you, DNA testers to trigger specific mods, ones that will make you so odd you don't dare show yourself outside of this facility."

Garik pictured Justin. Had he escaped before? Was that Garik's future? Was that what Rodheimer was showing him? He was being offered two choices, prison or more mods—and then likely still prison.

"So, Jantzen's out?" The question seemed important to Chad.

"Yes." Garik didn't say more. Was this a trap, a set-up so that he would disclose the man's location? If so, he wasn't falling for it. "I'm catching overtones of your voice. Is that possible?"

"You're timber wolf, so possible. Good about Jantzen, and for whoever else got out. If they're captured again—" Chad stopped and closed his eyes, his chest shuddering. When he calmed, he said, "Don't give anything away. Rodheimer still wants them back. He will chase them and do to them what he's done to me."

"Jantzen will protect—"

"He can't. Rodheimer will modify them all. Jantzen, that's a different story. He's hard to hold and hard to modify." Chad chuckled. "We all wish to be Jantzen."

Jantzen, bad guy or good? Garik was so confused. He didn't know right from wrong anymore. And was Chad sure he was part timber wolf? What Garik didn't know could fill a basement, even the one under Corona Tower, as big as it was.

— II —

o, you may get your wish after all."

Rodheimer slammed the door back, yanking his passkey from its interface. His presence swept into the room, a tidal wave of gigantean proportions. He dominated, overshadowed, blocked out all light. His fingertips sparkled with fireworks. Anger rolled from him like a summer storm.

Garik was truly frightened. The man had said he absorbed static electricity, but he was pulling all the electricity from the room. It was coming out his fingertips. Who would die today? He hoped it wasn't him.

"Whose wish?" Garik managed to squeak out.

"Fool, boy! Is that what you wish me to believe? Don't play me the idiot. You are as transparent as glass."

Following him, a whimper of a woman trailed in. Her black bangs didn't quite hide the scar on her forehead. Garik remembered her from the event on the mall, Angelica. Jantzen had stopped to speak with her.

"That one. I want him with us." Rodheimer thrust an arm Chad's direction.

"He is under treatment, Director." She said the words but without conviction, almost as if she realized she had no authority in the Director's presence.

"Under *my care*. This whole facility is under my care. I authorize his treatment, and I am *unauthorizing his treatment*. Bring him. Everyone is to gather in the Lobby." Rodheimer was a black cloud of storm-thrashed weather threatening to inundate the research facility with his fury as he forced his way through the door and disappeared.

The lights in the room buzzed and came up to full strength. Chad caught Garik's eye and raised his deformed eyebrows.

Garik felt he had been yanked by Weston Rodheimer's leash and now had reason to doubt that even Houdini could find his way out of the basement complex of the Corona Tower. They had only managed before with Jantzen's help. Now, he was somewhere in the city, his freedom guaranteed.

What call did he have to help Garik now? And if Weston Rodheimer could be believed, he wouldn't want to. He had used Garik for his escape, and now that he was free, the man would disappear like smoke in the wind.

Purple smoke in the wind, but smoke nonetheless.

Garik's head spun, and he knew if he didn't find some answers soon, it might spin right off, and he'd never find himself again.

CHAD WAS being prepped for additional surgeries. Rodheimer's announcement changed that. His IVs were disconnected, and when Angelica helped him get dressed, his legs were marked with sharpie lines to guide the surgeon.

Clear the floor. If the surgery had been in progress, would they have left the scalpels sticking out, the blood flowing, even as Rodheimer dragged Garik in for his object lesson? Behave, or this is what I'll do to you?

Or had the leader of the project simply known the timing, and he'd organized their visit at the opportune moment? A power play. That seemed more like him.

Hunched into the powered chair and covered with blankets, the merged bat-man became an adroit driver, navigating obstacles like he had them mapped out in his head, nearly clipping corners and barely missing people, but never making a mistake.

Stupid me, Garik realized. Echolocation. Of course, he never collided with anything. The world *was* mapped out for him in his head. No wonder Rodheimer wanted what he had to offer. A spy or soldier who knew within millimeters the exact location of every person and every object that could be a weapon? Even in the dark? Brilliant!

Human hybrids were flooding the main lobby by the time they arrived. Angelica hadn't joined them, and most if not all the participants exhibited some sort of genetic abnormality. Ears, cranium, nose, limb size, coloring, or hair. Many could pass for human, given the correct clothes, but even more would never pass in a face-to-face encounter. Not with wings, true fangs, or skins of scales.

Garik located Marina Bruni, Marisa's older sister. She reminded him of Marisa, until she turned. One half of her was aquatically adapted. On the other side of the room, Hector Mascari scampered in. Garik hated to admit it, but scampered was the only term that described how the man, er, mouse entered the room.

Okay, not a mouse, but more rat than man. He had changed since Garik first met him. Now, he was more rat-like than ever.

The others—well, he didn't know many. The group he'd helped escape, Jantzen had organized his life around them, and there'd been little place for breaking the ice with anyone else.

Now he began to think that maybe he should have. Whatever was going on, nothing like this had occurred since he'd been part of the research facility's team, albeit after being kidnapped and forced to be on the team.

He searched for Van Hermoso, T'Wana Dolalas, Devon Maye, even Leah Fortinier, aka Nurse Ratchett, and Doctor Jimenez. Nowhere. The attendees were a select crew, only those initiated into the human-hybrid program.

Garik suspected this was bigger than he'd bargained for. He didn't want big. He wanted one floor up, the elevator doors opening to the Corona Mall, and he wanted to run as fast as he could, turn the world to rainbows if that's what it took. See ya' lata' Miz Kournikova, I'm outta he-ah.

With the last of the hybrids exiting from the elevators from the lower floors, thick blast shields erupted from the floor, shooting up before every door, effectively sealing them in the lobby. Steel shutters rumbled over the skylights. From the sound, they were blast-proof, also. A stage rose from the center of the room, and from it appeared a metal room etched with designs. The door was sealed with a circular steel handle four feet across, like the hatch on a submarine. It began to unscrew. A door perhaps a meter thick broke free, and out of the darkened space emerged Halo Sunchaser, gleaming in ivory and leather. Her hair was bound at the crown but erupted into a wild cacophony of midnight fireworks, tossing wildly at every move.

The mood of the hybrids fell quiet, a spaceship landing on a foreign world, no one quite sure what was going to happen.

Or maybe they were, Garik allowed, and that was the reason for their silence.

Either way, Rodheimer stepped out, his demeanor blacker than before, as if his anger might erupt into a downdraft that would destroy anyone within range.

They were all within range.

A glass case floated out after them, suspended by some force Garik couldn't see. Magnetics. Wires. Trickery or magic, it didn't matter. The people around him seemed to know exactly what it was. Rodheimer reached a hand, lightning shot forth striking the case, and the lid opened. Sunchaser stepped to it as if performing a ritual, and she lifted a sword by the hilt. The heel of one hand was wedged against the pommel, and the other against the guard. It flashed and gleamed under the lights.

"The sword!" Rodheimer let the words rumble from him, and they flowed across the crowd with a visible ripple, a holy object they all recognized and understood. "Who dares the sword?"

This time, his voice sandblasted his listeners, and all

around Garik, eyes fell to look at the ground. Garik wanted to belt out, Marisa, I've seen it! The sword, it's real. You were right all along. I'm looking at it now!

"Yes, hear it from me. I want there to be no mistake nor misunderstanding. We are minus twelve of our kind. Look around you. See who they are. None are worth your consideration, for all were failures with no opportunity for advancement in our plans. Does anyone not understand?"

"I understand," the hybrids said as one.

It's a cult, Garik muttered, his heart pounding. Are these people brainwashed? Rodheimer had said the participants in the program joined willingly, but this was freaky. Who would behave like this?

"Say it again," Rodheimer demanded.

"I understand." The words came louder.

"Even my second has betrayed us. The outside world will never give us freedom until we force them to bend their knees. The time is coming. Our time is coming. One day, just not yet. The redemption in today's events is that one has returned to us."

Garik looked around for the one of his friends who had escaped with them and returned. Paolo? Joanie? He couldn't see either of them. Before he could cover the rest of the list, he heard his name.

"Garik Shayk, an example for us all."

Garik wanted to sink into himself. He dreamed of Houdini, not being an example for these people. He wanted his freedom, not praise. His goal was to reunite with Marisa, not be separated from her. He was jerked out of his self-examination by an eye-watering flash from the stage and a thunderclap of lightning-laced air.

Electricity—lightning, if you will—linked Rodheimer with the sword Sunchaser held aloft, and it began to glow with a fierce light. Then Rodheimer broke the connection, leaving the sword aglow with energy and power.

"Who else dares to attempt to undermine me? I am the authority over all of this, over all of you. If you think you are different, that you can flee, rethink your plans."

Rodheimer seemed to swell in the brilliance of the sword, one side of his body pulsing with light, and the other bathed in darkness. He reached behind his head, wadded the collar and yoke of his shirt and coat in his fist, and tore them from his body, slinging them to the side. His eyes blazed white and his shoulders and chest were covered with masses of silver-black fur.

"I am the Silverback. This is my domain. Cross me, and the electrified sword will find you!"

Halo Sunchaser let out a yell of triumph, and electricity leaped from the end of the sword and splayed out over the ceiling. It seemed it would never end.

— 12 —

odheimer's manic display of white-eyed and silver-encrusted power was only the outer crust of the deep-fried ball of anger that splattered the hybrids before he was done.

The sword was awesome. Garik admitted that. He admired the pulsing rivulets of power that sprinted across the ceiling, even as the spectacle of the theater playing out around him shocked his grasp of what he thought he knew.

The Silverback. He had been fixated on it, certain it

might be him. Perhaps it still was, or would be at some point in the future. Rodheimer's words to him had suggested as much initially. *"You and me, just alike."* Yet Garik didn't think so. At least not yet. There was no way he could shoot electricity from his fingertips, so surely Rodheimer hadn't meant it literally. *"Third generation ... recognizably human ... gain their confidence."* That meant intent, desire for power, the love of being different and walking over people because of it. That was how he saw them the same. Yet how had Garik dreamed himself as the silverback? What had sucked him into that black hole and shot him out the silverback wormhole on the other side?

Garik's fog of harsh self-appraisal cleared enough for him to pay attention to several hybrid goons organizing themselves around the outside perimeter of the room. Small groups had begun to clump together, cliques of like-minded individuals, those who had skills or modifications to give them common ground, or maybe they shared goals, like escaping the basement complex, and they wanted the perceived strength that could only come from numbers. Only the outer individuals would get eaten, er, lashed by Sunchaser's sword when things got serious.

True enough, people were cut from the herd, peeled away a person at a time. Sunchaser and Rodheimer flowed from the raised platform into the surrounding sea of people, and the nearest mutant hybrids gave them room, like schooling sardines avoiding a larger, predator species. The smaller group of guilty individuals was banished to the platform, hemmed in by two of the goons.

The sword continued to shimmer and pulse in Sunchaser's hand, although its deadly power no longer crawled along the ceiling. The threat was clear. Hide, and you will be found. Lie, and you will be punished. Plot, and you will be plundered and divvied up to the most deserving recipient.

Chad was the proof of that.

Garik imagined his legs, and he cupped one hand around each thigh. He wanted to keep them. Now was his time to decide the best way to do that. Escape? Both Rodheimer and Chad had sliced that coconut in half, and all the milk inside had drained away with the electrical bath washed over the ceiling by Sunchaser's sword. Cooperation? The very idea curdled in Garik's stomach like eating soured custard on rotted meat.

"Which one will get it?" Chad's voice through his modulated box interrupted Garik's fractured thoughts.

Garik jumped. "Oh, it's you. I thought you would be back in surgery by now."

"No one's leaving till the Director gets his revenge."

"Revenge? What have they done?"

"Plotted, perhaps. Maybe nothing. If he feels crossed, however, someone has to pay."

Oops, Garik thought. I plotted. Hey, I'm still plotting. Can they read minds, too? If so, I'm in for it.

"You worried?" If Chad's electronic voice could chuckle, it would have.

"I did leave and was BolaWrapped." *A second time.* "If he makes anyone pay, it's likely me."

"Nah, that's not Weston. You cross him, or simply don't measure up, and he writes you off. Come back repentant, and he forgives all. I suspect he sees you as repentant. After all, you are back. Good on ya', mate, for finding a way to survive this nightmare without having your legs and arms cut off."

"Yeah, sorry about that. And good on ya'? What does that mean?"

"Aussie. Well done. And you had nothing to do with my punishment, so don't worry about it. Just keep yourself in one piece, whatever price you have to pay. Like the Director says, now's not the time. You wait for it. You'll know when it's time."

"Time for what?" Half-speak. Garik wished people in this facility would spit out what they meant.

"You'll know when the time comes." Chad looked at him hard for a minute before his wheelchair whirred, and he moved away.

On the platform, a tribunal of sorts was in play. A kangaroo court. A mock trial, determined to winnow out a guilty party, even if there wasn't one. That's what Chad had seemed to suggest. Garik tried to hear what was going on, but the volume in the room had gradually increased to an uproar. People were now yelling, some defending, and others accusing. One person was finally separated from the rest, leaving five people huddled together and the other standing alone. Accusations flew, and she didn't try to defend herself. Those in the group of five pleaded, two crying, and one fell to his knees.

Rodheimer and Sunchaser ignored them all. The Director nodded as if a decision had been made, and he turned his back on the lone individual, crossed his arms, and looked over the crowd. At one point, his eyes settled on Garik as if to say, "Watch this, boy. This will happen to you if you don't mind yourself. I'm the Silverback, and in this place my word is law. I carry the power of life and death, and that includes you." Then his eyes moved on.

Garik shivered.

The scene was made worse when Sunchaser let out a yell, aimed the sword at the accused individual, and let its power fly. Electricity leaped from the end, surrounded the unfortunate victim, and seemed to disassemble the person molecule by molecule, atom by atom, until only the light from the sword filled the space. The sword winked off. Finally, the room was silent, with everyone too overwhelmed to speak.

"Payment has been accepted." Rodheimer's words rumbled from him. "The Silverback has spoken."

Sunchaser returned the sword to its glass case, and

they returned to the vault-like metal chamber, which began to sink into the floor. The five people remaining on the platform fell at the spot their friend had vanished and wailed in despair.

Around the room, the doors revealed themselves, and the skylights with their views of the black sky overhead blossomed from the ceiling. The human hybrids throughout the room milled around for a time before drifting away through doors and into elevator shafts. The mood had been pancaked by the removal of one of their number, dropping a cloud of blackness over the room.

Garik hadn't known her, but he felt it the same.

"AH, MR. SHAYK."

Garik turned and his world grew blacker. Not Airman Vang. He grimaced and forced politeness from his throat. "Airman Vang."

"I'm looking forward to spending time with you, Mr. Shayk. I am to be your escort to your quarters."

"My quarters ... and where would that be?" He hadn't considered where he would stay. After spending the afternoon in the Director's penthouse and splitting the evening between the hospital and this gruesome sideshow in the lobby, Garik had expected to be locked into a cell on Level 5, if he was given any leniency at all.

"And where would that be." Vang turned the

question into a sneer, more a statement than a simple response to the teen's inquiry. "You tell me, Mr. Shayk. It has only been a day, and you couldn't stay away. You, ahem, *chose* to return of your, ahem, *own volition.* Did you think you would suddenly move to the penthouse with the Director?"

Garik watched the man's mixed message of a face, his eyes more Cambodian than Caucasian, his skin more freckled than fierce, and wondered what the Airman had in for him. His height? Garik now saw that he was an easy half a foot or more taller than the neatly turned-out Airman.

"My old quarters, sure, if you would like." Garik wondered how that had escaped him. If they hadn't cleaned out all his stuff, at least he would have fresh clothes. Still, all that effort to escape, damaging Kevin's van, the disastrous meeting with Marisa, and now a woman dead. And he was back right where he started. "I don't have my passkey any longer."

"You will not need it. I recall the door's locking mechanism has been sliced away. A terrorist act by your fellow terrorist. Pardon, you have been absolved by the Director. Alyna is the likely culprit. If your door won't lock, you won't need a passkey, will you, Mr. Shayk? You can wander in and out at will."

Garik wanted to say, *You can stop calling me Mr. Shayk. That's my father's name.* But he didn't dare. The man was making a point. Garik might have returned, but he had bucked the system, or at least had chosen to flee with those who had, and Vang wasn't giving Garik the benefit of the doubt that he hadn't intended to stay out of the Tower's clutches.

He was a runaway who had gotten caught and was playing to the Director's soft spot, however Garik had managed to reveal one. Guilty in intent was guilty in fact, even if the Director had praised him before everyone present.

That got Garik thinking. How did Airman Vang know what the Director had said or done with the blast doors in place? There had been no one present except the participants in the human-hybrid program. Someone was revealing his hand, and that someone was Airman Shan Vang.

They used Vang's passkey to take the elevator down a floor. Garik's quarters were a short walk through somber and oppressive spaces that only days before had seemed generous and inviting. After his taste of freedom, Garik wasn't sure he could ever think of the underground research facility as inviting. Prison, no matter how luxurious, was still a prison.

At Garik's quarters, the door was closed but clearly not sealed. One side reflected the claws on Alyna's hands. Garik expected the Airman to accompany him inside, perhaps assign him a guard or, heaven forbid, remain to guard him himself. The thought was worse than mortifying. Instead, the Airman stepped aside and said, "Good night, Mr. Shayk. I will wait until you are inside, so if you don't mind." He motioned with his hand.

Garik pushed through the door and pressed it closed, sealing off Vang and refusing to turn on the lights with the Airman watching. He hit the switch and got a surprise.

"Hey, hey. Lights, please." Someone stretched out on his sofa yanked a blanket over a blond head of hair.

"Devon?" What? Why would the facility's rec planner and coordinator be sleeping on his sofa?

"Yeah. Lights, if you don't mind."

"Of course." Garik hit the switch. "What are you doing here?"

"I'm assigned to be your conjoined twin. I hope you like recreation." Garik heard the man shifting on the sofa, and he was surprised that he could see him sitting up, even in the dark. "So, what went on at the meeting?"

"At the meeting?" Garik groaned. Would he ever stop repeating other people's questions to him?

"You and the weir—er, the program participants. You know, you special people. What do you people do on the main lobby when the walls seal all you off?"

"We weirdos do weird stuff, like play with swords and things. You know, fireworks. You know what those are?" Garik felt the trauma of the evening boiling over into anger, and he struggled to contain it. Devon wasn't the enemy, and if anything, he considered him a friend. It wasn't fair to take his frustrations out on him.

"I'm sorry. I forget how you hear things, pick up on stuff others can't. Can you see me in the dark, too?"

"Yeah. Start wearing pajamas to bed if you're sleeping on my couch."

"Right-o, kiddo. That's funny." Devon laughed.

"I mean it." Garik's eyes had fully adjusted, and the man had bed hair and wore brightly patterned boxers covered with Christmas trees. "And Christmas isn't for another month. Turkeys are for Thanksgiving."

"For real? They are passing out night vision now? Finally, something useful." Devon fell back onto the couch and kicked the blanket up and over him. "I'll think about it, okay, kiddo? Just leave the lights off when you come through, and we'll get along fine."

That left Garik to question his place in the scheme of this facility that the Director should value his return so highly. He certainly wasn't the next silverback. Rodheimer had clarified that.

That led him to his big question. If Garik wasn't the silverback, then what was he? He didn't have that answer, but as long as he was trapped here, he might as well cooperate long enough to find out. Once he did, Houdini time!

If he could find a way to escape the Tower's clutches once again.

In Book Five, Garik Shayk's friends besiege Corona Tower, rocking the foundations of the behemoth corporation.

The Glass Siege

Book Five

The Human-Hybrid Project

Garik Shayk has been inducted into the secretive Human Hybrid Project buried deep within the Corona Tower. He has managed to escape once, but this time, his imprisonment is secure. Or is it? Garik's friends have not forgotten him. Social media protests threaten to erupt into citywide riots.

The Human-Hybrid Project

Addictive!

A 10-book series you won't be able to forget. Explore each upcoming book, the characters, and more at www.thehumanhybridproject.com.

Book 1   Book 2

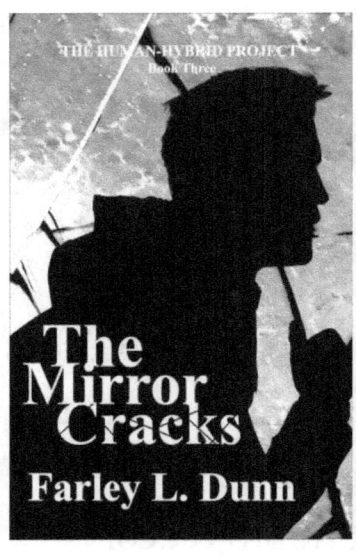

Book 3

Book 4

Book 5

Book 6

Book 7

Book 8

Book 9

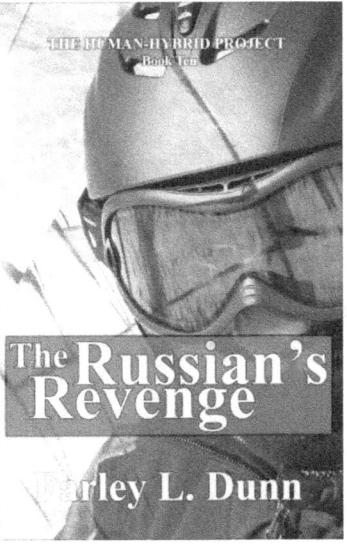

Book 10